ABOUT THE AUTHOR

James Warden was a teacher for forty years, and retired in 2006. He now enjoys his retirement as much as he enjoyed his time in the education service, and is catching up on those things which he left undone and ought to have done – in particular, his writing. He writes every morning between nine o'clock and noon, for thirty-six weeks of the year.

He is fortunate enough to be able to act in several Norwich theatres – the Maddermarket, the Sewell Barn and, with the Great Hall Players, at the Assembly House – and this experience informs his writing. His stage adaptation of Laurie Lee's *As I Walked Out One Midsummer Morning* was performed at the Sewell Barn Theatre in November 2009. His original play, *Letters From a Boy in the Trenches*, which was based on the letters of a WW1 soldier, was performed in Marchington, Staffordshire in 2015.

James is married – for the second time – and lives in Norfolk. He and his wife travel as much as possible. They have visited Italy (where they were married in 2002) several times, Canada, Bermuda, Egypt, India, the Czech Republic, New England (USA), Poland, Slovenia, Antarctica, the Falkland Islands, Alaska, the Galapagos Islands, and Australia. They have also taken several holidays in various Mediterranean resorts – the basis for his first novel, *Three Women of a Certain Age*, which was published in July 2010.

During his years in education, he wrote about twenty play scripts for children. These included the one that formed the basis for his children's story, *The Great Gobbler and his Home Baking Factory at the North Pole*, which he wrote in 1982 and published in December 2010.

He has three sons by his first marriage and they inspired two of his novels – *The Vampire's Homecoming*, which was published in 2011, and *The One-eyed Dwarf,* published in 2012. With them and his first wife, he also travelled to the southern states of North America, France, Germany (West and East), Estonia and what was Czechoslovakia.

WRITING BY JAMES WARDEN

Letters From a Boy in the Trenches
*(Adapted from the letters home of Sydney Harrison
and performed by the Marchington Amateur
Dramatic Society in November 2015.)*

<u>The Bingham Detective Stories</u>
Bingham's First Case
Bingham and the Runaway Wife
(To be published in the summer of 2019)
Bingham and the Odd Couple
(To be published in the summer of 2020)
Bingham and the Minister's Clerk
(To be published in the summer of 2021)
Bingham and the Traveller's Daughter
(To be published in the summer of 2022)
Bingham Down Under
(To be published in the summer of 2023)

BINGHAM'S FIRST CASE

BY

JAMES WARDEN

Grosvenor House
Publishing Limited

The right of James Warden to be identified as the author of this
work has been asserted in accordance with Section 78
of the Copyright, Designs and Patents Act 1988

The book cover picture is copyright to James Warden

This book is published by
Grosvenor House Publishing Ltd
Link House
140 The Broadway, Tolworth, Surrey, KT6 7HT.
www.grosvenorhousepublishing.co.uk

A CIP record for this book
is available from the British Library

ISBN 978-1-78623-314-1

To
My wife, Lindy,
for her continued patience
when I walk about the house
talking to myself.

Chapter One
HAUNTED TO THE GRAVE

"My failure to find that little girl will haunt me to the grave."

Bingham looked at the speaker and gave his old friend a sympathetic smile. The two men were standing by, or rather leaning, on the gate that opened into the orchard adjacent to Bingham's home. They had just eaten a celebratory meal cooked by Lina Bingham: a meal in honour of the speaker's retirement. Ex-Detective Chief Inspector Simon Brockie had wanted to round off the meal with his story of the one failure above all others that saddened him beyond comfort: six years before he had been one of the officers in charge of the investigation into Natalie Beddoes disappearance.

Lina, seeing that Brockie's wife, Aileen, considered the story inappropriate to the occasion, had suggested that they should "see to the dishes", leaving the two men to walk down to the orchard where the bees were still buzzing contentedly around the landing boards of their hives. A rare spate of warm weather in an otherwise dreary summer was about to produce a heatwave, and both men could feel the coming change in the air. Bingham glanced at the apple blossom, anticipating the taste of the thick, amber honey the bees would produce from the nectar: honey with just a hint of apple.

Both men stood silently: in common with many of their sex, neither felt the need to speak in the company of an old friend. Bingham was sipping contentedly from a glass of his favourite whisky – Old Pulteney from Wick – and Brockie felt he was keeping the bees at bay, exhaling smoke from the cigar Bingham had offered when they reached the orchard. Brockie's wife did not approve of him smoking – an attitude that both amused and annoyed Bingham.

Neither spoke but each shared the same thought. What had happened to Natalie Beddoes? Little girls deserved better than to disappear at the age of six, never to be heard of again; a flash of anger appeared in Bingham's eyes. Thinking about her and remembering the photograph that had dominated the front page of every newspaper in the country for weeks, and thereafter occasionally for years, as the fruitless search took place, Bingham felt guilty at his own good fortune. He had four healthy children, all grown up and safe and sound, while the family of the little girl with the snub nose and the wavy, black hair would mourn her loss until their dying day. Not knowing: he imagined that was the terrible thing.

He looked behind him at the light of the summer evening fading over his home – the one-time farmhouse inherited from Lina's parents and still called Bob's Farm after a favourite childhood pet. Soon his three dogs would appear, harrowing him for their last walk of the day, and the thirteen cats would begin to stir from under the long table in the huge kitchen as they prepared for their evening prowl. Bingham realised how contented he was, what a cosy life he led, and felt guilty for the second time that evening.

"Let's stroll down to the barley field," he said, giving a loud whistle so that the dogs would know, "With all this dry weather, the apples may be a tad tiny this year but I think we'll have a golden harvest."

He and Lina had sold the land to a farmer who looked after it following the death of her parents, but they retained the house, the orchard for his bee hives and some of the older outbuildings. Bingham and his wife would often walk the fields at night, savouring the joy of living in the countryside, remembering a childhood she felt to have been "privileged". Summer was the time when the lanes were full of flowers and blossoming grasses: hedge-parsley and chervil, buttercups, the buds of the ash unfolding, the pungent sweetness of the elderflowers.

Bingham placed his whisky glass on the gatepost and wandered to the old farmyard, where their pond was sheltered by the oak whose leaves were fully opened. Lina was the gardener. It was she who cleared the pond at the end of each autumn; the water lilies with their white petals and yellow centres were to her credit, not his. Their moorhen – they always talked as if the bird belonged to them and knew it – glided with her fourteen chicks, now half-grown but still with their fledgling down, to the safety of the far side of the water. Bingham was always amazed that she kept her brood so safe from the hunting instincts of thirteen cats.

A haywain was ending its days by the side of the pond. His children had used it for whatever their imaginations suggested as they grew up, and Bingham often sat on its shafts to remember and think.

"Sit down, Simon," he said, "enjoy the remains of your cigar while you tell me about the disappearance of Natalie Beddoes."

Brockie smiled gratefully at Bingham. They had first come across each other when Bingham, during his life as a schoolteacher, intervened on behalf of one of his pupils. It concerned the matter of a silly 'dare'. The boy had been goaded into stealing sweets from a corner shop. He'd owned up but not before the police had become involved. Bingham didn't feel that shaming the boy to his parents would achieve anything useful and that a criminal record would actually be harmful. He considered the proverbial clip-round-the-ear to be far more sensible and to the annoyance of the young policeman investigating the case had approached Brockie, who agreed that discretion was the order of the day: discretion being that quality of a true leader that gives them the courage to toss the rule book in the waste bin.

Brockie had admired Bingham's "concern for the young man," and later, as they became acquainted through the work of the local Crime Prevention Officer, his ability to listen. In Brockie's view the world was awash with talkers but unequally blessed with listeners.

"Do you remember anything about the case?"

"One image sticks in my mind," replied Bingham, "There was a bicycle involved, wasn't there, and one of the papers had this story that the first person to come across the scene of the girl's disappearance found the back wheel still spinning."

"It was Natalie's grandmother, and she swears it was true."

"I put it down to the fevered imagination of a journalist."

"No, no. In many ways it appeared to be the key to solving the mystery, but we were unable to make anything of it. What seemed a central clue led nowhere. Natalie disappeared a few hundred yards from where she lived and almost on her grandmother's doorstep. It was a summer's day, much like this one has been: warm, sunny, farm labourers in the nearby fields, children out playing, holidaymakers on the beach. She was cycling from her own house to her nana's, along what amounted to a footpath. Do you know Aldewich?"

"Yes. Lina and I often drive there. The dogs enjoy the sea."

"Then you'll know there are only two ways in or out of the village. With the North Sea to the east, you can only travel north-west to Sizewick and, eventually, Eastwold and Lowestoft, or south-west to Easleton and, eventually, Ipswich. The immediate roads out of the village either cross Easleton Heath or pass through Aldewich Forest."

"And you think that Natalie was taken out of the village?"

"Right after her disappearance we scoured the forest and heathland. Since then, helicopters have been used in ground searches and the RAF has used reconnaissance aircraft to photograph the area."

"But it is a huge area covered densely by trees and gorse."

"That is true, and we continue to keep an open mind."

"What happened on the day of her disappearance, moment by moment?"

"Natalie, along with all her family – her father is a farmworker – was an early riser. By 7.30 that morning, they'd all had their breakfast and were about their daily business. Alan Beddoes, the father, had left for work, and Emma Beddoes, the mother, was busy hanging out the washing. Natalie and Moira – that's her sister and she was two years older than Natalie – were playing in the garden. They played there with their dolls all morning.

"The Beddoes house was once a tied cottage for farm labourers, and it stands in a row of similar cottages along what amounts to a private road, although it is open to the public as a footpath to the clifftop walk. Occasionally the girls would wander off along this road because it gives access to the grounds of Whitefriars, a medieval monastery, where a neighbour keeps her horses, which she allows the girls to ride."

"And Mrs Beddoes was comfortable with this arrangement?"

"It's a small, Suffolk village, George – much like this one where you live – and the children are free in a way they would never be in a town. Yes, Emma Beddoes was pleased for her daughters to wander into the pasture. Natalie and Moira had no fear of animals of any kind."

"And they went into the pasture on that particular morning?"

"Yes – to show the horses their dolls."

Bingham could imagine his own daughters doing much the same thing. He glanced over to the pond where they had played together and remembered gathering in their toys after they had gone to bed at night.

"Mrs Beddoes gave them their lunch in the garden, the weather was so fine, and they sat with their dolls to eat it. This would have been at 12 o'clock. Emma Beddoes is a stickler for meal times. After lunch, the sisters quarrelled about something – Mrs Beddoes wasn't sure what and Moira wouldn't say – and Moira went to her bedroom and Natalie wandered off to see if one of their friends along the row of cottages would come and play.

But they were all out for the day and she returned half an hour later."

"Were there any holidaymakers about during that time?"

"Several walked to the clifftop."

"Do you know if Natalie spoke to anyone?"

"She said she had spoken to a man with a dog and a lady with a baby in a pushchair. We asked through the local paper for those people to come forward but neither did."

"How did she spend the rest of the afternoon?"

"She was at a loose end with her sister not wanting to play and so Mrs Beddoes asked if Natalie would like to take some chutney she'd made to her nana. It would give her the chance to have a ride on her new bike. The bike had a little basket on the front where Natalie sat her dolls. Natalie said she'd go but that she'd like to change into her 'best clothes' first. We wondered why this was, but Mrs Beddoes said she liked to wear a certain dress when she went to see her nana because her nana had liked it."

Bingham sighed at the many memories of his own daughters dashing back upstairs to their bedrooms for a last minute, sudden, change of clothes. It struck him that Natalie Beddoes must have been a rather personable six-year-old.

"Mrs Beddoes wrapped the jar of chutney in tissue paper and placed it in a small carrier bag before putting it in the basket of Natalie's bicycle. The little girl wheeled her bike proudly to the front gate, which Mrs Beddoes opened for her. She then waved her daughter off and watched as Natalie cycled across the road to the footpath. It was the last she saw of her. Mrs Beddoes went inside to phone her mother to say that Natalie was on her way, and then got on with some ironing. She said the time could not have been later than 1.30, and the timing is critical at this point.

"We tried to construct what was happening in this small coastal village during the next five minutes: who was where and what they were doing.

"On one side of the footpath is Whitefriars meadow. A family was crossing there with their dogs – two, black Labradors. No one in the family could remember seeing Natalie on her bike. The other side of the footpath opens onto three gardens. No one was at home in the first two and the gates are padlocked from the inside. A family was sitting over lunch in the third garden and they did notice their dogs run to the gate at one point. They couldn't be sure whether it was Natalie who attracted them.

"Gwen Davis, Natalie's grandmother, was in the bathroom when the phone rang and it took her a few minutes to get to it. She then hurried up the driveway of her bungalow and found Natalie's bike abandoned just outside the gate, which was open, and off the road. The wheel was still spinning."

"Natalie's bicycle was examined, I suppose?"

"There were no prints on the bike other than Natalie's and her family – the mother's, the sister's, the father's and the grandmother's."

"And the dolls and the chutney?"

"The dolls were still in the basket. Being heavier, the jar of chutney had rolled onto the ground. Strange as it may seem, Mrs Davis actually picked it up and replaced it in the basket before propping Natalie's bike against the gatepost. She then hurried out into the road to look for

Natalie, but there was no sign of her. At this point, the road from Easleton forks and leads down into the village: the right hand fork going directly to the beach and the left passing the church before joining the road to Sizewick or Eastwold and, eventually Lowestoft. She then rushed back in and phoned her daughter, Emma Beddoes.

"Mrs Beddoes phoned the local police officer – there was a station at Easleton in those days. The officer at the time was John Russell. He noted the time of the call at 1.39. He phoned his section sergeant at HQ and then immediately got on his bike and cycled to the scene. It's a matter of two or three miles. He arrived at 1.59.

"He passed no traffic on the road. It later transpired that a couple in a white Ford Fiesta had driven into Aldewich along the same road just before him. They, too, passed no one on the road as far as they could remember. They did remember passing Mrs Davis's driveway and seeing the bike propped against the gateway.

"A search was already underway when John arrived. Mrs Beddoes had roused an elderly couple who lived next door and they were checking Whitefriars."

"Is the monastery still used?" asked Bingham.

"Yes – as a retreat. There was a group in residence at the time, but they were all at lunch when Natalie disappeared."

"Go on."

"Mr Beddoes was at work and since he didn't believe in mobile phones his wife was unable to contact him except by phoning the farmhouse, which she did. It took him some while to receive the message and it was after 3 o'clock before he arrived back home.

"In the meantime, John Russell had cycled the village looking over hedges and into fields. In one, he disturbed a courting couple – teenagers – but they had neither seen nor heard anything."

"How close were they to where Natalie disappeared?"

"They were in a field on the road that forks to the left and comes out by the church: probably four or five hundred yards away from Gwen Davis's gate and about the same distance from the churchyard, which John examined next. It was inconceivable that a child of six could have wandered any further in the time that had passed between her leaving home and her nana finding the abandoned bike; however, there was the possibility that she had made her way along the right-hand fork and so John Russell made his way to the beach, stopping off first to ask at the village museum. There's a fish restaurant on the beach and John enquired there but to no avail.

"By now, it was clear that Natalie's disappearance must be viewed in a very serious light. John Russell phoned his section sergeant a second time. Sergeant Meredith then informed divisional HQ in Ipswich. By early evening, detectives and uniformed officers were interviewing holidaymakers, villagers, the family and anyone else who might have been in the vicinity They also conducted an immediate but thorough search of banks and fields, barns and outhouses. It was approaching midsummer's day and so the search continued late into the night.

"Mr and Mrs Beddoes remained at home, waiting by the telephone on our advice. They sat there throughout the night, hoping for a call and yet fearing one.

"My superior officer, Detective Chief Superintendent Gazeley, was the senior officer of the investigation, and I was called in to take charge of the Incident Room, which we set up in the village museum."

"Was Scotland Yard involved?"

"No. There's a great deal of misunderstanding about the role of the Yard," replied Simon Brockie with a degree of asperity in his tone, "The Yard is only called in if it is felt that the local force cannot cope with the investigation. It's generally recognised that small forces with their limited experience and resources might find themselves severely stretched by a major crime investigation, and the facility to ask the Yard's help is always available: however, that is on the understanding that they are called in within 24 hours of the discovery of a body or the instigation of the investigation. We had no body, no evidence that a major crime had been committed and DCS Gazeley felt confident that we could handle the investigation; but it was clear from the outset that we faced a daunting task.

"The countryside around Aldewich is vast: rolling heathland and dense forests. From that first day, we all had a sense of foreboding. Was Natalie Beddoes dead or had she been abducted? If the latter, was it by someone locally or had she been taken from the area? If locally, then there might still be a chance of finding her alive, but it was a slim one. If she had been taken from the area then the logistical and organisational problems would be immense. Senior detectives on the case feared the worst.

"I was in close touch with Alan and Emma Beddoes from the beginning, and I've spoken with them many times over the subsequent years. Those very key initial 24 hours passed and there was no sign of Natalie, and so experienced, specialist officers were called in. People were re-interviewed; Natalie's bike was examined and photographs were taken of the surrounding area. I set up an enquiry and search unit in the Incident Room for receiving and assessing information and documents. It was clear now that we would proceed upon the painstaking grind of asking question after question, hoping to inspire more questions that might offer a lead. It was check and double check all the way, examining evidence, appraising witnesses, following up information and probing theories.

"The first searches had concentrated on the immediate area, and we re-covered that old ground before moving on: dogs were used, divers searched the coastline and specialist equipment was brought in to probe for a grave. We examined crevices and corners in every outbuilding for miles around. The RAF offered the services of their air-sea rescue helicopter. It swept across Easleton Heath and beyond, it swooped low over Aldewich Forest, it circled fields and hedges, lanes and side roads, it hovered over back gardens and farmyards, caravans and holiday sites, unoccupied buildings and derelict buildings but found nothing. This main search went on for a week and we got nowhere."

The ex-policeman's voice appeared almost on the verge of hysteria, and so Bingham reached into his pocket for the case of cigars and offered Simon Brockie another. He smiled and refused. The light had now faded into darkness and several of Lina Bingham's cats could be seen by the green light of their eyes. His three dogs, having dispensed with any idea of a walk, were settled by his feet near the shaft of the haywain. The two men sat silently while Simon gathered himself together.

"I don't want to weary you with the details of the investigation, George. It's just good to be able to talk this through for one, last time ... The art of investigation is to explore possibilities, confirm the negatives and eliminate all explanations of what might have happened until only one remains."

"Were there no reported sightings?"

"Dozens – there always are – but none that amounted to anything. Natalie was seen with a man in Sizewick and with a man and a woman in Lowestoft; she was seen boarding a train – again with a man – at Darstoft Halt; she was seen getting out of a grey van with a man in Eastwold; a bus driver saw her boarding a Number 5 bus in Ipswich. The press was busy sensationalising the story, and people were desperate to help.

"A man was arrested in Blytham, which is just up the road from Aldewich, because he was asking detailed questions about the search and people were suspicious. He was a holidaymaker. We checked him out and searched his room but he had a cast-iron alibi. He'd been drinking in the Lord Nelson on the lunchtime that Natalie disappeared and the landlord remembered him.

"Two elderly ladies who live in a house off the right-hand fork said they heard a scream at around the time Natalie vanished. This report was never resolved. We asked whether they could remember hearing the sound of any vehicles on the road but they were adamant they heard nothing of the kind."

"If Natalie was snatched from the entrance to her grandmother's driveway, marks must have been left on the ground."

"On the basis that no one can enter of leave a place without leaving something, however small, in that place – the much-loved forensic principle of exchange? There was nothing."

"What results did your alleged sightings turn up?"

"The man who boarded the train at Darstoft Halt was with his granddaughter. Several people confirmed the sighting on the Number 5 bus, thereby supporting the driver's belief that it was Natalie, but enquiries in the Foxhall Road area of Ipswich produced nothing."

"And the grey van in Eastwold?"

"Was never traced, and no one in the village recalled seeing one."

"How many cars were on the beach carpark that day?"

"Scores, on and off. We sent out an appeal through the press and many people came forward saying that they had been on the beach but no one could give information that produced a lead."

"You said earlier that the investigation had tried to establish where everyone in the village was at the time of Natalie's disappearance. Where were they – especially the family and those within the immediate vicinity?"

"The mother and grandmother offered each other alibis. To doubt one would mean doubting both. The father was certainly on one of the harvest fields when he received the message that his daughter had disappeared. Mavis Tilt – the owner of the horses – was out riding with her husband: again, they provide an alibi for each other."

"No one else saw them?"

"Not that we could determine. They were riding the bridle paths across Easleton Heath. They own a riding school out that way."

"Where do they live?"

"The private road in front of the Beddoes cottage leads to an even more private one along which are a number of second homes. These are residences that were previously cottages but which have been knocked into one dwelling. The Tilts live there. It gives access to the meadow that borders the footpath."

"Does anyone else live there permanently?"

"Not at the time, but a writer has since moved into one of them. She took up residence about two years after Natalie disappeared. That would be in 2011."

"What does she write?"

"Crime novels: not fiction but real crime."

"And the monastery opens directly onto the road that leads to Easleton?"

"Yes."

"But you're sure no one left the monastery during the lunch hour?"

"We questioned everyone independently. Some took a stroll after lunch, but usually in groups of two or more."

"You've questioned the staff?"

"They were all busy in one way or another."

"Even the gardeners?"

"Yes."

"What about the road that leads down directly to the beach – the right hand fork from where Natalie disappeared?"

"There are several houses there. The one next to Gwen Davis's is the home of Gaye Hewitt. She lives with her son."

"How old is he?"

"A year older than Natalie. He'd be 13 now."

"But they didn't play together?"

"No. They both attended the village school, which is several miles away in Middleham, but he generally played with the few other boys in the village. The mother was home at the time Natalie disappeared. The boy,

Joseph, was playing with the landlord's son in the yard of The Smack."

"And the other houses on that stretch of road?"

"The owners were out for the day. We checked where and when," replied Simon Brockie with a smile, quite taken aback by Bingham's barrage of questions, "You'd have made a good policeman, George."

"I doubt it. A love of paperwork isn't one of my virtues. Who lives on the other road: the left hand fork that goes down to the church?"

"There's a derelict farmhouse. The owner does some haulage work with an old truck. It would have been a horse and cart not long ago! He's a crusty old boy and we couldn't get much out of him or his wife. Salt of the earth type but doesn't like authority. He was a great support to the Beddoes following Natalie's disappearance, though. He visited them every day. He's a friend of Alan Beddoes.

"The only other house is the vicarage. The present incumbent is the Rev John Crisp. On the first Sunday after Natalie's disappearance, he held a Communion service at St James's Church. There was hardly a soul in the village and the villages around who didn't attend: believers, agnostics and atheists alike. They all prayed for Natalie's safe return. She'd prayed there with her family and attended the Sunday school."

"Junior Church!"

"Sunday school! You'd like John Crisp, George. He's like you – a maverick, and he prefers the old nomencla-ture. He works hard in his parishes – cycles everywhere. He still places flowers in the church every week as a symbol of hope for her return."

"Where was he at the time?"

"In the church. They were having the roof done and life was rather fraught even for a country vicar."

"So, there were workmen around?"

"We questioned them all. The firm was most cooperative."

"Who were the courting couple?"

"The lad was Mike Peck. The girl was Olive Freeman. They still live in the village. They were married in St James's."

Bingham stretched his aching back and rose from the shaft of the haywain. Being old had its compensations but stiffness in the joints wasn't one of them. He was unsure why he'd asked so many questions. Was it to encourage Brockie to talk so that once and for all he could get the matter outside of himself and in the open, where it might disperse and allow him to enjoy an otherwise well-deserved retirement?

He looked down at the dogs who were watching his moves intently. They'd missed their walk and Bingham felt guilty. Dogs like routine, as did Bingham; both were flummoxed by its absence.

"Let's complete that walk by the barley field," he said to Brockie, "The dogs will appreciate it."

"We've been rather a long time," replied Brockie, "My wife will be expecting to go home before long."

"Lina will keep her entertained. It won't hurt her to wait," was Bingham's retort.

Chapter Two

THE SMACK

Much to his annoyance, Bingham heard the dining bell before he had finished checking his hives. Years before, he had rigged a large ship's bell outside the kitchen door to call his children in at mealtimes, since they were often playing far from the house. Lina had objected that it didn't seem right to summon your children by bell, and Bingham had invited her to come up with a better idea, since by the time he'd walked round to find them the meals would have qualified as frozen food. She never had, and it now gave her great pleasure to summon him as he had once summoned their offspring. His annoyance was mollified by the fact that he could actually hear the clear tones of the bell: Bingham was partially deaf, a blessing he'd inherited from his mother.

It was late June – the time of year known to beekeepers as the June Gap: a time when the spring flowers are fading and the summer ones yet to bloom. Bees would often find forage to be scarce and Bingham was feeding them with a sugar-syrup solution. He was disdainful of anyone late for meals and so he laid the feeder over the hole in the crown board and rapidly replaced the roof before hurrying to one of the outhouses where he removed his bee-suit.

"Sorry if I'm late," he said, panting slightly.

"You're not," replied Lina, "I rang early in case you were with the bees. I've yet to scramble the eggs – and don't curse under your breath, Bing. It's unbecoming."

His wife was the only person in the world who called him 'Bing'. At first, he'd found it annoying, as had been her intention, but the habit was now one of the ingrained idiosyncrasies of their relationship, and Bingham would have been upset had she called him by any other name.

"You were up early."

"I couldn't sleep," he replied, taking a huge gulp from the cup of scalding tea she placed on the table before him.

"You were thinking about the little girl?"

"Yes."

"You were muttering about spinning wheels and forks."

"Was I? Yes, that spinning wheel. I was also thinking about our children, especially the girls. Do you remember how we used to let them cycle along the private road to the house? I say 'private road', but the public use it as a footpath and a bridleway. Anyone could have snatched them, and we'd have come across their bikes, the back wheel spinning where it had fallen. It doesn't bear thinking about. Were we careless parents? Should we have kept them fenced in?"

"I don't think so, and neither do you. They won't find the little girl, now – not after all this time – will they?"

"Someone, somewhere, knows something," replied Bingham, "It's that simple."

After breakfast, Bingham returned to his hives to complete the feeding programme and check the brood chambers. It had been a good year so far: the brood was plentiful and the supers full of honey. He was expecting to collect at least 30 pounds from each hive if the weather continued to pick up. Lina would be in her element cooking: roasted figs with gorgonzola and honey, honey-glazed vegetables, traditional honey cake, honeyed yoghurt and spicy chicken wing marinade came to mind. Not that they ate meat anymore, but honey made the substitutes a little more interesting. There would be plenty to sell at the Northfield church fete and his sons, in particular, would appreciate the mead.

As these images rolled through his mind, Bingham's thoughts were elsewhere and it was with relief he heard the dining bell. He knew that coffee was brewing on the stove and that he could share his thoughts with Lina. She always had something useful to say.

"Can you imagine how her parents feel?" he said, kicking his shoes off at the kitchen door, "Have they ever slept since that dreadful day? I doubt it. Not real sleep, not the sleep that knits up the ravelled sleeve of care. To know would be dreadful, but not to know even more so."

"So you are still thinking about that little girl. I thought you would be. You never said a word during breakfast, not even to compliment me on the beetroot and apple bread. I don't think you even noticed what you were eating."

"I remember Natalie Beddoes' photograph in the paper at the time. It's not right, Lina, that people should feel free to snatch children from their homes."

"Why don't you spend a few days in Aldewich, and put your mind at rest."

Bingham looked up at his wife as she spoke, and smiled. He found it wonderful to be married to someone who could read his thoughts: at least, he found it wonderful at times.

"Take Pippa with you. She'll enjoy the exercise and you won't look as odd as you would on your own."

Pippa was their black Labrador, and younger than the other two dogs. Since they'd rescued her, she had been exceptionally fond of Bingham and accompanied him everywhere except to the beehives.

"Would you mind? Can you manage without the car?"

"No I won't and yes I can. You're a brooder, Bing, and I find your brooding irritating. Going to the village will get it out of your system."

"You don't think I'll come up with anything?"

"After all these years – what, six, isn't it? – and where Simon Brockie and his colleagues failed?"

"But I'm not a policeman," replied Bingham, "Over time, loyalties change, memories slip out of control and guilt digs in. I wonder if The Smack does bed and breakfast."

"They do, and I've booked you a room looking out over the sea – and yes, they take dogs," replied Lina, with a smile.

It was early evening when Bingham arrived in Aldewich. The bar of The Smack was paved with flagstones. At the far end of the small room, three men sat at a scrubbed, wooden table. At first, Bingham thought they were discussing business but soon realised that they were passing a laptop backwards and forwards between them, playing a game. He thought it rather a retrograde step from draughts, dominoes and cards. The barman gave him a knowing smile and nodded at his holdall.

"Your wife phoned earlier. The room's ready. Would you like a drink?"

"I'll have half a Ghost Ship."

"Will you be staying long?"

"Perhaps a day or two. Have you a bowl of water for my dog?"

"I'll bring one over."

Bingham glanced round the bar during this exchange. At a small, solitary table by the lattice window that overlooked the road sat a woman reading *The Guardian*. She was smartly dressed in a brown, pinstriped suit; a matching brown trilby was placed on the seat beside her and a gin and tonic on the table in front. The barman caught Bingham's look and mouthed "dyke", with another knowing smile.

"My name's Lewis Paulton," he said, extending a wet hand across the bar, "I take it you're here on a walking break. I know the area well, the footpaths and so on. I have a map you can borrow."

"I may take my dog for a walk in a moment," replied Bingham, "I understand there's a footpath that runs alongside the monastery grounds. Can I reach that from the clifftop? I'd rather stay off the road."

"You can reach Whitefriars from the clifftop. Will you be requiring a meal this evening?" asked Paulton, bringing both Bingham's beer and Pippa's water to a table in the corner.

"Yes, I think so. How long have you run The Smack?" he said, realising that unless he asked questions there was no point in his being in the village at all.

"We came just after the little girl ... just after ... excuse me a moment. May I take your holdall up to your room?"

Paulton more or less snatched the holdall from the floor and dashed off through the door by which Bingham had entered. As he did, a laptop player rose from the table and left abruptly, leaving his beer unfinished and throwing the bar a filthy look.

"Alan!" called another of the players, but too late to stop his friend from leaving.

Bingham noticed the smartly dressed woman peer over the top of her newspaper and smile. Bingham didn't like the smile: there was a sneer in the curve of the lips.

By the name called out, Bingham assumed the man hurrying from the bar, at the landlord's slip of the tongue, was Natalie's father. His sympathy went out to him: living in a village that wouldn't forget could only rub grit into the soreness of the wound. He looked up to see the friend towering over him. The man was red-faced and burly with a shock of grey-white hair jutting in spikes from his head.

"You people," he growled, throwing angry looks at both Bingham and the woman in the pin-striped suit, "Why can't you leave us well alone?"

"Are you the carter?" asked Bingham.

"What's that to you?"

"A chum mentioned you. He said you didn't like authority but were a good friend to Mr and Mrs Beddoes."

"I dare say, but that's none of your business whoever you are," he snapped and hurried from the bar.

"What's going on?"

The speaker, a fat woman in her forties with an oily skin, came in from behind the bar. "Amos – has Alan gone? Lewis is sorry. He didn't mean to upset him."

"He's got a big mouth for a landlord," replied the third laptop player as he closed the lid and left the pub.

"Oh dear," sighed the woman, looking at Bingham, "I'm Teresa, I'm the landlady. You must be Mr Bingham. How do you do. Would you like to go to your room?"

"No, I think I'll take Pippa for a stroll," replied Bingham, offering his hand, which Teresa Paulton shook warmly, before disappearing through the door behind the bar.

As he left, the smartly dressed woman said, without looking up from her newspaper, "You certainly know how to clear a room, Mr Bingham."

Having no suitable response, Bingham pretended not to hear the remark; impending deafness has its uses. He stepped into the corridor and walked out through the front door with Pippa.

He felt the heat immediately: the promised heatwave was on its way. Bingham crossed the road in the wake of the man called Amos, who was striding towards the beach. On the footpath, he unleashed Pippa and she settled into an easy walk at his side. Only a few minutes passed before they reached the pitch-black hut that served as a fish restaurant known by all as 'Percy's' after the man who had first owned and created it. Percy's served fish fresh from the Aldewich beach. Fishing along and off the whole of the Suffolk coast had declined rapidly but there were still pockets of perseverance where longshore fisherman plied their trade and Aldewich was one such place.

Amos passed behind the restaurant and made towards what Bingham supposed was his boat. Nets strung across the gunwales had been drying since morning, and more hung from the racks. As he reached the boat, Amos turned and saw Bingham.

"Are you following me?"

"Yes," replied Bingham, "I wanted to apologise for the upset caused to Mr Beddoes."

"Won't your fault," grunted the fisherman, "It were Lewis Paulton: him and his mouth. They came to the village at the wrong time, they did."

"Just after Natalie disappeared?"

"They were round and about afore then. They brought bad luck and it's hung over us like a thundercloud ever since."

"You don't think they had anything to do with her disappearance, do you?"

"Who's to know? What I do know is that they were round and about."

The phrase must have been one he'd used many times, thought Bingham, and means no more to him than it does to the truth of the matter.

"Will you be going out over the next few days?" he asked.

"The tides roight," was the curt reply.

"Then I'll pay you a call when I leave."

"You're not hanging around then, like some?"

"Like?"

"Her that was in the bar – the dyke."

Amos laughed as he spoke, just like a child who used what he'd always thought to be a naughty word. Bingham realised it was new to his world: not just the word but the idea.

"Doesn't she have a house here?"

"She does now. Always nosing around, always asking questions."

"What kind of questions?"

"About Alan's daughter. But she ain't a policewoman. She's a nosey parker. She writes things."

"Does she often sit in the bar?"

"Whenever she's waiting in The Smack. There's a room for the women, but she don't use that – not her."

"Do you know who she's waiting for?"

"Him that comes up from London or maybe her up the road," said Amos, and then added, with a laugh, "Gaye Hewitt. That's her name."

"Her son, Joseph, plays with the landlord's boy, doesn't he?"

Suddenly, Amos squinted and gave Bingham a hard look.

"You know a lot for a stranger."

"A friend of mine was involved in the investigation. It haunts him to this day that Natalie remains missing."

"You're not a copper."

Bingham wasn't sure whether the remark was a question or an assertion.

"No, I'm not," he replied, and then added, "but neither am I a writer. What chances do we have of ever finding the little girl, do you think?"

"They were looking everywhere," replied Amos, "but never in the roight place. I'm saying no more."

With that remark, he strode along the beach watched by Bingham, who – had he been a policeman – would have brought the fisherman in for questioning. Instead, he called Pippa to him and strolled off along the road.

The slight hill took him up and past the entrance to the monastery. Further along the road, he came to the fork and realised he stood within a few feet of the spot where Natalie's bike had lain, its wheel spinning. He looked beyond the spot and down the driveway of what must have been the grandmother's bungalow. Had Gwen Davis been in her front garden she must have seen the moment Natalie arrived, but she'd been in the bathroom. Wasn't that always the case when the delivery man knocked on the door?

Behind him, the signpost indicated 'Beach and Car Park' and 'The Smack, Aldewich'. The other arm pointed to Blytham, Eastwold and St James's Church. Bingham wondered whether the vicar might be in his front garden soaking up the warmth of this beautiful summer evening. Even for a reputedly compassionate man there must be moments, six years on, when he forgets the little girl who had disappeared. Some Christians would see it as the will of God, of course, but Bingham didn't think that attitude applied to this particular one.

He realised he must have passed Gaye Hewitt's bungalow and strolled back to look, but the six foot, solid wood, gates were shut and he could see nothing. Not wanting to return to the pub as yet, Bingham continued walking along the road until he came to where it turned towards Easleton. To his left was what Brockie had called 'an even more private road': the sanctuary of second homeowners and the writer. Judging from what Amos had said, she must be the woman who was in the bar of The Smack. What was her name? Had he been told and forgotten? His failing memory was becoming more common these days, but he was sure he'd have remembered.

Bingham turned along the road that was little more than a metalled track. The houses here may once have been farm labourer's cottages but they were far more than that now: porches, garages, extensions and landscaped gardens had turned them into luxurious dwellings. Some were open to the road; others hid behind high, beech hedges. He wondered where the writer lived and whether she'd returned home since he left the pub. Bingham was aware that he had no right to ask anybody questions, but felt that the writer would talk willingly. He was irritated with himself that he had feigned deafness at her remark. He might have learned more just sitting and listening; but then, of course, he would have missed what Amos had to say.

He returned to the fork in the road and made his way towards the church, passing first the field where the courting couple had heard nothing and then the derelict farmyard of the carter. Here he paused, hoping the man might accost him. Beyond the battered gates was an old barn full of what appeared to be junk, but there was no movement to suggest anyone was about. Bingham moved on and came to the church. Nothing stirred among the graves, which offered their own kind of peace on this warm, summer evening.

Bingham walked in through the south porch, looking for Natalie's memorial. He found it on the sill of a south facing window: a bunch of Madonna lilies framing a simple request: 'In your prayers, call to mind Natalie Beddoes, who disappeared from this village in June 2009, and remember her family who hope and wait'.

Bingham left the church in a hurry: suddenly, his own daughters were vividly in his thoughts and an unreconciled anger in his heart.

Back at The Smack, he ordered two half pints: one of Ghost Ship and the other whose name his eyes could not make out but which came from Cliff Quay Brewery in Ipswich.

"Will you be eating, Mr Bingham?" asked Teresa Paulton as she served him.

"In a while," retorted Bingham as he downed his first half in one pour and reached for the second.

"Lewis and I arrived just as the little girl was taken, you see, and it's been held against us ever since. It makes no sense, but the two events are linked in the minds of the villagers."

"But they still drink here?"

"Oh yes, but Mr Beddoes isn't angry like his friends. It's just that he tries to shut it out and then something happens to remind him."

"Such as your husband's slip of the tongue?"

"Lewis will apologise in his own way. Mr Beddoes wouldn't want a direct apology."

"No, of course not. The carter seems to be an angry man."

"Inbred like a lot of these villagers. They say his mother and father were cousins. His heart is in the right place, although you mayn't believe it, but he's unpredictable. Hail fellow well met one day and doesn't speak to you the next. You learn to take him as he comes."

"But a good friend to Mr and Mrs Beddoes?"

"Oh yes. He was as kind as kind to them when the little girl disappeared. The vicar put on a special service, you know, and it was the only time I saw Tony Ship with tears in his eyes."

It was the first time Bingham had heard anybody use the carter's name, and it seemed friendly enough, posing no threat to man or beast. Bingham came from the town himself – Wolverhampton in Staffordshire – and had a limited knowledge of country people who appeared to be a race apart. There were villagers in Northfield, a small village to the north of Ipswich where he now lived, who would bestow enormous affection on their dogs and then, quite happily, blast the head off a rabbit.

"I'll have the fish pie, please," he said, "and another half of that Cliff Quay beer. I can't read the label on the pump."

"The Full Steam Ahead? That's a summer beer. We've their Classic Bitter, too, in the other bar. That's a nice drink."

"I'll have a half of each."

How quickly we drop into the everyday, thought Bingham, but it's the everyday that keeps us sane. He imagined Emma Beddoes ironing as she had been doing the moment Natalie disappeared, and Alan Beddoes putting his back into the work of the coming harvest. How else but by embracing the ordinary could they hope to survive.

Bingham remained in the bar all evening until he walked Pippa at ten o'clock, after which he went to his room. It was pleasant enough: the leaded window, overlooking the marsh and the sea, closed for the night with floral-patterned curtains that slid along a wooden pole on rings of wood. Teresa Paulton had put a vase of flowers on the centre of the sill: lilies again, reminding him of everlasting life. The sad irony was not lost on Bingham.

He settled Pippa on the bed he'd brought with him, and she watched him undress, fold his clothes carefully on the hanger and place them in the wardrobe. Bingham's obsession with tidiness was a source of laughter at home. He unpacked the clothes from his holdall and selected a suitable drawer for each, before phoning Lina.

"Yes, a great deal," he said, in answer to her query, "The landlord upset the girl's father and that led me into conversation with several of the locals … No, I've seen Mr Beddoes but not spoken to the family … I'm not sure … You think so? Perhaps I'll drop by tomorrow. There's a woman writer who lives in the village. I've a feeling she may be a source of information if she's done her homework … Yes there are lilies in the church … Pippa's fine … Good night. Love you."

Lina thought he should approach the family, but Bingham wasn't convinced that would be decent: many know-alls must have upset them many times. There were always cranks in cases like this one: the mediums, the dowsers, the ones with strange 'powers', the religious maniacs. All wrapped up in themselves; promoting distress in others for their own edification.

It was a comfortable bed and Bingham slept well, waking at six-thirty as he always did but, this morning, with Pippa's wet nose poking his foot that protruded from beneath the duvet. He pulled on yesterday's clothes and took her for a toilet walk. On the beach he saw no one. The line of the cliff stretched far into the distance, obscured slightly by the early morning mist. Pippa enjoyed the chill of the morning and splashed about in the surf; Bingham stumbled about on the pebbles, wishing he was younger.

He returned through the back door of the pub to shower and dress afresh. It was eight o'clock when he went downstairs and found Teresa brewing tea.

"Would you like a cup? It'll be a while before breakfast is ready."

"Thank you. I'm in no hurry."

"What are you doing today?"

"I don't know. Your husband's faux pas led to some interesting conversations yesterday. Perhaps I'll be as lucky today."

"Lewis has his uses," she replied, with a laugh, "You might try talking to that Jenny Inkpen."

"The writer? Is that her real name?"

"I don't know. I've seen it on her books. That's all."

"The day that Natalie disappeared, your son was playing with the son of a friend of hers. Is that right?"

"Joseph Hewitt was here but not playing with our son. We'd only just arrived. It was the son of the previous landlord. You don't think children were involved in her disappearance, do you?"

"I don't think anything. I'm just trying to place where people were at the time."

"Well, Lewis and I were being shown the ropes, so to speak. I think we can vouch for each other and the previous owners who were with us. What would you like for breakfast?"

"There's no chance of eggs royale, is there?"

"I think we can manage that for you, but you may have to make do with a sliced roll instead of muffins."

Chapter Three

THE UNLOCKED DOOR

Bingham tucked into his breakfast vigorously: he'd always enjoyed his food. Pippa sat at his feet, her Labrador eyes watching his every mouthful, and he handed her a piece of the salmon when he'd finished.

He was just contemplating his next move, which he felt might take him to the fateful footpath, when he was roused from his thoughts by a tap at the window. The beaming face of a priest looked in on him and nodded towards the door, which Bingham opened.

"Are you the gentleman making enquiries about Natalie Beddoes?" he asked, "Don't look puzzled. News travels fast in a village. I bumped into Amos Pritchard last night. He's a bell-ringer. I imagine you're a private detective, and I may be able to help. Well, not so much help as give good advice. I'm John Crisp, by the way, as if you hadn't guessed that already."

"Sit down, Rev Crisp …"

"John, please."

"John. Would you like a cup of tea?"

"A vicar never refuses a cup of tea, Mr … Mr … I'm sorry, I don't know your name."

"Bingham, George Bingham. Please sit down and I'll ask Mrs Paulton for …"

"No need for that, Mr Bingham. I heard the Rev Crisp and I'm brewing a fresh pot," called Teresa Paulton from the bar.

Bingham disliked being rushed; he was a contemplative man, and the vicar's verbal onslaught had quite overwhelmed him. He was glad when the pot of tea arrived and Teresa engaged John Crisp in conversation while she poured them both a cup. After she'd left, he took charge of the conversation.

"I'm not a private detective," he said, "or any kind of detective. I'm here because a friend of mine was engaged on the case and is distraught at his failure. I came because I have this vague – possibly vain – idea that something might be turned up if I nose around."

"Quite: a new mind, a new line of enquiry, a new initiative. The Beddoes have always welcomed any chance of finding their daughter, and that's what I've come to tell you. I've spoken to Emma Beddoes this morning and she would like to see you."

"Really?"

"Yes. I thought you might hesitate to approach her out of a mistaken sense of propriety and because of Alan's hasty exit yesterday, but that would be wrong. Hope springs eternal in a mother's breast, George."

"But Mr Beddoes feels differently?"

"Yes. Alan feels…"

"If you'll finish your tea John, perhaps we could whistle and ride."

Despite his attempt at workplace humour, Bingham was aware that his tone was curt; but he had no wish to discuss the Beddoes in a bar already filling with other residents.

"Of course, of course! How thoughtless of me. We'll continue our conversation at the vicarage."

On their way, they passed the museum and, while the vicar talked about the village's history, Bingham watched his new acquaintance. The Rev Crisp was a small, wiry man – probably pugilistic, thought Bingham, when his views were questioned or his sense of rightness outraged. A man in love with his people and his work; a man tied to cups of tea and the annual fetes; a man consumed by his way of life.

The vicarage was Victorian: solid, grey, outstanding with its bay windows, classical portico and ironwork. An impressive residence designed for just that purpose, but somewhat out-of-tune with this modern vicar.

"My wife, Eileen," said John Crisp, breaking his historic flow to introduce his wife who opened the door to them.

Eileen Crisp had just removed her apron. Bingham knew that because he saw it slung over the coat stand as they entered. She stopped patting her hair and held out her hand, which Bingham took. He'd always found vicar's wives to be either screwed down tight or all over the place; he judged Eileen to fit the latter mould, judging from the boots, shoes, umbrellas, clothes and children's toys distributed throughout the large hallway.

"You'll have to excuse the mess," she said, "I didn't realise John was bringing anyone home. He dashed off without having his breakfast."

"I wanted to catch George before he set out and I had to see Emma first."

"Quite," said Bingham, as reassuringly as he could manage, concerned to save the vicar an earful after he left, "I rather invited myself, Mrs Crisp. The bar was filling with residents."

"Would you like a cup of tea?"

"That would be most welcome," he replied, wondering how much more of the stuff he'd be obliged to drink during the course of the day. He never had more than one cup at home, although Lina never drank less than three: the one he took her in bed, a second with their breakfast and a third to settle her stomach after the meal.

The kitchen was large, cool and welcoming on a morning already showing promise of the heatwave to come. It was cluttered with the detritus of mealtimes – the previous night's supper judging from the casserole dish and the morning's breakfast saucepans and cereal packets. There was no sign of children but Bingham could hear several voices crying out in the garden.

"Alan Beddoes has accepted that his daughter is unlikely to be found. He has taken what people describe as the philosophical approach. He feels that talking about her loss, constantly 'digging up the past', as he expresses it, is harmful to their other daughter, Moira, and a burden on them all. You mustn't suppose that he is an unfeeling man. Quite simply, he cannot bear the pain on a day-to-day basis and he buries it deep within him. Not talking about it, not reading about it are his ways of coping."

"If he would let himself cry once in a while, it would help both him and his wife," suggested Eileen Crisp as she poured Bingham and her husband their cups of tea from a large brown pot.

"How do they get on with the rest of the village?" asked Bingham.

"He drinks a lot with his cronies – Amos Pritchard and Tony Ship – but Emma keeps herself much to herself," replied Eileen.

"You don't approve?"

"I don't see how it helps either of them."

"Eileen is a get-it-out-in the open kind of person," laughed John Crisp.

"Do they attend church?"

"Every Sunday, without fail."

"And Emma always helps out with the fetes and so on. It's as though she feels safe behind a stall. She also comes to the WI, but everyone there knows her, of course."

"How does the village see them?"

John and Eileen Crisp exchanged glances that were not lost on Bingham, who looked down at the table so that his eyes offered no challenge.

"Opinion is divided. Most people are sympathetic but there are those who are openly hostile."

"In what respect?"

"They consider the Beddoes were at fault, that a six-year-old child should not have been out alone and…"

Bingham looked up as John Crisp paused.

"They are some who think the Beddoes know more than they're saying," said Eileen, continuing her husband's disclosure, "The world is full of spiteful people."

Bingham's walk from the vicarage took him past the field where Mike Peck and Olive Freeman had been canoodling on the day of Natalie's disappearance. Bingham came late to love, but could remember vividly its initial intensity; when he'd listened to Brockie's account of the investigation it didn't surprise him that they'd heard nothing on that fateful day.

The gate wouldn't budge – its weight had sunk it into the ground – and so he climbed over and into the meadow, while Pippa waited anxiously behind the bars. It was only a small meadow, perhaps enough for a cow in calf that needed to be kept close to the farm, and Bingham wondered where the young lovers had hidden themselves. Surely they would have one ear to the road in case they were disturbed? The meadow curved away from Tony Ship's derelict farmyard, and there was a place or two in the far corner where the teenagers might have found some privacy; but in that case they would have been very close to the driveway of Natalie's grandmother. Would the intervening years have loosened their memories?

It was still early morning in the village, and the holidaymakers had yet to arrive. Bingham could hear the twittering of birds, a few voices that seemed far away, the clank of wood on metal, farm machinery in the field to his left and, perhaps, the odd vehicle on the beach carpark. He wasn't sure: all sounds were muted these days, as his deafness progressed.

He seemed impelled to visit the Beddoes first, and the obvious way was along the footpath, which lay just beyond the fork in the road. Bingham didn't want that walk. It didn't feel right to travel the same footpath as Natalie, but in the opposite direction. There must be another way, he thought, and he walked on to where a side road took him by a barley field.

The large garden of a guest house, The Old Forge, was to his left. A notice below the sign offered 'Afternoon Tea in the Garden' between 3.00 and 5.00 at a cost of £5: English scones, butter, jam and cream and a pot of scalding tea. Bingham usually enjoyed his second cup of the day at that time, and perhaps a third. He thought of Lina and wished he was home.

Pippa sniffed her way down the road and Bingham followed. Winding his way through the woods that eventually hung precariously on the edge of the clifftop, he came to the village end of the 'even more private road' and so to the one on where the Beddoes cottage stood.

"Come in, Mr Bingham," said Emma Beddoes, opening the door as soon as he placed his hand on the gate, "Never mind the dog. We like dogs here."

The kitchen was small and meticulously tidy. The floor was flag-stoned and glistened with cleanliness. A young teenage girl sat at the table. She looked at Bingham wearily.

"Aren't you going to say hello to Mr Bingham, Moira?"

"Hello, Mr Bingham," she said in the flat 'must I?' voice of her age.

"Hello, Moira. You must be … fourteen."

"Fifteen next birthday," she replied, and smiled.

"Off school today, are you?"

"She's not been very well, Mr Bingham. Moira's under the doctor."

"Can I go out, Mum? I can't stay in all day. I won't go far."

"See that you don't. If you're well enough to go out you're well enough to go to school."

The girl slid noisily from the kitchen and disappeared into the cottage. Bingham heard her moving about upstairs for a while. Eventually, an outside door slammed and there was silence.

"She'd have been a different girl if her sister was still with us. She's got no one now, you see – no one close, that is. Thank you for coming, Mr Bingham."

Bingham felt uncomfortable. He was intruding on the grief of these people: the father avoided him, the sister left as soon as he arrived, only the mother seemed welcoming. He looked at Emma Beddoes and smiled. She wore a wrap-around apron over a woollen skirt and a flowered blouse. Her hair was permed in a style that resembled the Queen's. She couldn't have been forty, thought Bingham, and looked like a woman well into her fifties. When children disappear, the lives of others are lost forever.

"The Rev Crisp said you would be pleased for me to come."

"Oh yes. Any ray of hope brings me a little comfort."

"I'm not a detective. I'm a friend of Simon Brockie's"

"The policeman? He was very kind. He's been back now and again to see us. Would you like a cup of tea, Mr Bingham?"

"No, thank you, not for the moment."

He didn't know where to begin. What question should he ask first? Natalie's mother looked at him, waiting for answers

"On second thoughts, I will have that tea," he said, and Emma Beddoes smiled with relief as she filled the kettle.

Once they were sitting at the table, she seemed able to talk.

"I blame myself. I should never have let her go alone. But she'd been so many times before. As a toddler, she would walk and my mother was always there to meet her. But even if she wasn't – she was old, see, and took a little while getting up the driveway – Natalie would wait or just go down the driveway on her own. It was so close to the footpath."

"Did anyone, other than your mother, know that Natalie was going to see her nana?"

"No."

"How often did she go? Every day, now and then, was it a routine?"

"She would often go and see her nana but not at regular times."

"So no one could have anticipated that she might have been at that place at that time?"

"No, no one."

Bingham was aware that his questions must have been asked so many times before, over and over again, and yet Emma Beddoes did not seem weary with them. She was crying but the tears did not show. She must have wept so much over the last six years that there were none left to run down her pale cheeks.

"What did you think when your mother phoned that day?"

"I didn't think, Mr Bingham. I panicked. I saw Natalie's bicycle and I ran up and down the road looking for her. She was nowhere to be seen."

"Did you notice anything or anyone along the footpath?"

"There were the dogs that belong to the people at the end barking at the gate. But I already knew she'd been stolen. She was nowhere to be seen, and Natalie wouldn't wander off on her own. She was a good girl. Someone had taken her."

"Who did you think it might have been?"

"I had no idea. We rushed down both roads …"

"Which neighbours came out to help?"

"Mr and Mrs Cooper. They're an elderly couple and live next door. And Moira. She was only eight at the time. I was shouting and crying at the same time. 'Not Natalie', I kept thinking, 'not Natalie. Please God, not Natalie'."

"But no other neighbours came out?"

"No one else was around."

"What about the people who were crossing Whitefriars' meadow?"

"I think they'd gone. I don't know about them."

"What about the people who owned the dogs who barked when you went down the footpath?"

"They came to the gate, but I don't think they thought it was serious and that we'd find Natalie."

"Were you still searching when your husband arrived home?"

"It was 3 o'clock before Alan arrived: he'd been up on the harvest field, and had to cycle home. We knew by then that Natalie had disappeared."

"Did your husband search for himself?"

"He went out into the meadow and had a good look and then came in to comfort me. He's a man of few words, Mr Bingham. He put his arms round me, which is unusual for Alan, and held me tight. We just stood here in the middle of the kitchen. He was howling inside himself, if you know what I mean."

"Yes, I can imagine."

"We'd failed her, see. It's a parents' responsibility to look after their children, isn't it, and we'd failed our Natalie. She was only six, God bless her. I kept saying that to him – that we'd failed her and he kept saying 'Shush. No, we haven't. Shush.' John Russel had arrived by then and he'd taken over organising the search, but we knew it was no good."

"Did you not think that she might be found somewhere in the village?"

"I didn't think at all, Mr Bingham – not then. I was so overcome with fear and helplessness."

"And later?"

"There are some funny people in the village, Mr Bingham. But no one like that – no one who would harm a little girl. We always thought Natalie had been taken from the village, and we still do."

Bingham knew next to nothing about the kind of people who abduct children. What he read in the papers was of little value, being sensationalised and of seven day's interest. He'd read no books on the subject, and like most people was ignorant. He imagined that a fever overtook them, a terrible desire to have a child, to take whatever risks were involved in the pursuit of that end in the need to satiate a perverted lust. Someone had told him, once, that you couldn't tell such a person from anyone else in the street. Bingham found that difficult to believe. He couldn't accept that such vileness wasn't visible in the eyes: the eyes being the mirror of the soul.

"Did anyone come to see you soon after Natalie's disappearance?"

"There was the police lady and people like that, and they were very kind but I didn't want anyone near me except the family. I was too upset, and when neighbours came I just wanted them to go away."

"Which neighbours came?"

"People we know from the church, Mr and Mrs Tilt who own the horses Natalie loved to visit, Mr Ship and his wife from down the road. The people you'd expect, really."

"How did they seem?"

"I'm sorry, Mr Bingham, I don't understand what you mean."

"What was their attitude? What did they say?"

"Bewildered would be the best word, I think. Nobody could understand."

"Were they sympathetic?"

Bingham wasn't quite sure what he'd meant by the question, and he could see the puzzlement in Emma Beddoes eyes. Why wouldn't they be sympathetic?

"The people we know well were. People like Mr and Mrs Tilt didn't say much, but they paid their respects. Some people were embarrassed and didn't know what to say but most were considerate."

"Was there anyone you might have expected who didn't come?"

"I can't say there was, Mr Bingham. A lot of people were at work. People came when they could."

"Have you ever received letters, postcards – that kind of thing – from anybody?"

"We receive loads. There was one lady who sent a card on every anniversary, and then suddenly stopped. We don't know why. We thought perhaps she passed on."

Bingham felt his line of questioning slipping from him. He'd had a thought: a notion of someone, somewhere resting uncomfortably with the guilt of another. If there was such a person, were they in the village on that day or did they become aware of what had happened later?

"Are you all right, Mr Bingham? Would you like another cup of tea?"

Emma Beddoes was watching him, her eyes full of concern.

"Yes. Thank you."

"You had a thought, didn't you?"

"I don't know, Mrs Beddoes. You don't have any of the letters or postcards you received, do you?"

"Oh yes. The police examined them and then brought them back."

"May I look at the letters?"

"They're in the parlour, Mr Bingham. I'll get them out. It would be best if you looked at them in there. They might pick up some crumbs in the kitchen."

The parlour was a small room stuffed full of furniture. A large table dominated the centre. A number of wooden chairs were placed under the window that looked out on to the side garden. A vase of flowers decorated the centre of the table. At one end there was an old, leather settee; in the corner, a cupboard from which Emma Beddoes retrieved a biscuit tin. She suggested he should sit down at the table and placed the tin in front of him.

Bingham sorted through the letters carefully. Most were messages of sympathy offered on the cards people could buy from their local post office or general store; others were handmade and beautifully decorated. It would have taken an absolute cynic to interpret these as anything but heartfelt condolences from people who had taken the trouble to write. Most were still in their envelopes and were dated from the time of Natalie's disappearance. Some were dated a year later, and a few several years later.

Bingham examined them thoroughly, especially the ones from the correspondent who had suddenly stopped sending. Emma Beddoes had been correct: they were from a woman. The cards were written in a meticulous, cursive script that suggested someone who had been educated no later than the fifties, after which the open italic hand replaced the style of the previous three decades. There was no address, but the stamps were franked 'Lowestoft'.

"They were a source of great comfort to me, Mr Bingham," said Emma Beddoes, placing a fresh cup of tea and a fruit scone – already spread with butter, jam and cream – beside him on the table.

"I'm sure," he said, turning back to the letters and cards.

The letters offered advice and counselling and prayers, often from people who had no idea what they were talking about. Bingham realised how annoyed he would have been at receiving such messages, but Emma Beddoes felt only gratitude.

"They helped to restore our faith in humanity, you see. It was good to know that people cared about Natalie."

"You go to church every Sunday, I believe, Mrs Beddoes."

"Call me Emma, please, Mr Bingham."

"George."

"We never fail to go and the Rev Crisp always remembers Natalie in his prayers. One lady from the congregation still visits us regularly whenever she receives the call. She'll appear on our doorstep at all hours of the day and night."

"Your faith hasn't been shaken by what happened?"

"It's been strengthened, Mr Bingham. God is our only hope and refuge now."

Bingham was not a man of faith, although Lina was a Catholic and they both attended the Anglican village church at Northfield: two apparent contradictions that had always amused Bingham.

Listening to Emma Beddoes, he understood that she was being polite to him because she was polite to everybody who offered sympathy or possible help; he also realised that her real trust was elsewhere. People like him might come and go with their theories, investigations and explanations: her God would go on forever.

He sifted through the remaining letters while Emma Beddoes watched. They came from the local MP, councillors, a journalist who had also visited them on several occasions; they came from writers who asked questions; they came from spiritualists, psychics and amateur detectives who offered solutions and accompanied their letters with maps

"We read them all, Mr Bingham. It didn't seem polite not to."

"You're a lovely lady, Emma – what my mother called 'the salt of the earth'."

"Do you think there's any hope, Mr Bingham?"

Bingham smiled but would offer nothing false, and he felt he was no further forward than he had been yesterday. Taking a last look at the cards and letters, he was just grateful that he wasn't one of the police officers who would have had to follow-up each one, sieving through the mass of correspondence.

He left Emma Beddoes standing in her doorway, waving him goodbye.

"Come at any time, Mr Bingham. This door is never locked – not until Natalie returns."

Chapter Four
HEARING NOTHING

Bingham once again avoided the footpath: he wasn't ready yet to follow Natalie on her farewell journey. He passed by and made for the cliff top walk, and it was there, while resting against a gate that overlooked the rear of the medieval monastery, that he met Moira again.

"Hello, Moira. Enjoying the fresh air are you?"

She blushed at the sight of him, pouted and flashed him an angry look. She was on the arm of a red-haired boy Bingham judged to be about seventeen. The boy leered and adopted a strutting pose when Bingham spoke. Neither responded to his pleasantry, but they could not pass Bingham who stepped away from the gate to greet them. He smiled a tolerant smile and waited.

"Is mum all right?"

"She's as all right as you'd expect. You must know more about your mum than me."

"People shouldn't keep bothering her."

"She doesn't see it that way. Your mum asked me to visit. She still thinks that your sister will return, and every interest is a new hope. Is that how you feel?"

"No, I don't think we'll ever see Natalie again."

"If that's to be the case, don't you want whoever took her to be brought to account?"

"What good would that do?"

"It would prevent the same thing happening to other children."

Moira shrugged. Bingham could see that she was eager to get home.

"What did you and your sister argue about on that day?" he asked.

"Nothing much. I forget."

"Was it about something that happened when you went to see the horses in the meadow?"

"No."

"Who did you meet there?"

"No one."

"Here, what right have you got to ask all these questions?" asked the youth.

"None, but you won't mind answering them, will you?"

"We might."

"You're hardly in a position to do so, are you?"

"What do you mean?"

"You know what I mean, doesn't he, Moira?"

"We didn't meet anyone," she insisted, "I snatched Natalie's doll, if you must know and threw it under one of the horses."

"And then felt ashamed about it?"

"Yes."

"Did Natalie tell your mum?"

"No... she was never like that."

"And you miss her?"

"Yes."

Moira was a little girl again. She burst into tears, pushed her way past Bingham and ran towards home. The boy went to follow her, but Bingham took his arm.

"She'll be OK. I want a word with you."

"I ain't got time. I've got to get to work."

"You can spare me a few minutes.

"Look, I've got to go. My dad will go nuts. We've got a job on this afternoon."

"Where is your dad?"

"In the pub."

"I'll walk down with you. I could do with a drink. It's been a long morning."

"You won't say nothing about Moira, will yer?"

"No, but I'll give you a warning, son. You be careful how you treat that girl. She's still a child. If anything happened to her, you'd be on the paedophile register before you could blink. Do you understand me?"

"Me – a paedo?"

"It's happened to other lads who got carried away in the heat of the moment, and it could happen to you."

"Moira ain't like that."

"I'm not talking about Moira. I'm talking about you."

Pete Marjoram left Bingham's side quickly when they reached The Smack, apparently concerned that his father should start asking questions, and Bingham settled into a seat by the bar window: the one occupied when he arrived by Jenny Inkpen. He'd yet to see her, but was putting off the pleasure.

He nodded to the Lewis Paulton who brought over two half-pints: one of Adnams Bitter and the other of Cliff Quay's Full Steam Ahead. He also brought a bowl of water for Pippa without being asked.

"Had a good morning, Mr Bingham?"

"Yes, I think I have."

"There's someone to see you. He's in the garden. It's Dave Cavendish. He's our local copper."

"I'll have the reed cutter's platter with the Suffolk Shipcord," replied Bingham, "when you're ready."

He felt tired, and had no inclination to listen to what amount to complaints from the local policeman. He was also aware of his own inadequacies. There were questions he'd meant to ask Emma Beddoes but hadn't liked to do so. What did she think of her husband's attitude six years on? Perhaps the answer was obvious: she was a loyal woman, and he'd proved supportive at the time.

He took a gulp of Full Steam Ahead and swilled it round his mouth. The thought of the cheese dish to come cheered him up: beer and cheese was an unbeatable combination. A quiet lunch, perhaps a doze in his room and then he'd be ready for an afternoon of asking more questions.

"Mr Bingham, I'm PC Cavendish. I'm pleased to meet you."

Bingham felt no such elation, but stood politely as the police officer entered the bar and shook the his hand.

"Will you have a drink?"

"Not on duty, sir."

"Oh come on, man. It's lunchtime. You'd accept a coffee, wouldn't you?"

"A coffee would be welcome, sir."

That wasn't quite what Bingham meant, but he let the matter drop and nodded to Lewis Paulton, indicating a cup and saucer in mime.

"My name's George, by the way. You can drop the 'sir'. What can I do for you, Dave?"

"I'll come straight to the point … George. I understand you've been asking questions about the disappearance of Natalie Beddoes?"

"Just a moment! Can we find a quiet spot in the garden? This bar is soon to fill with holidaymakers."

The garden was pleasant with wooden picnic tables and borders of hydrangeas and tamarisk. From the spot they chose, under a chestnut tree at the far end, Bingham looked out over the marsh. A mild sea breeze took the heat from the air. He felt he could sit there forever.

"Go on."

"I wondered what your interest was, sir – George."

"I'm a friend of Detective Chief Inspector Simon Brockie."

Bingham could see that the name meant nothing to Dave Cavendish but had created a strong impression. Sensing trouble, he pushed home his advantage.

"He has just retired, but was one of the investigating officers on the case. His failure to find Natalie remains one of the great regrets of his life. I'm here, late in the day, to see if… something turns up."

"Do you think that very likely, sir?"

Bingham noticed that the respectful tone was back. He'd heard such a tone from headteachers many times in his career as a mathematics teacher, and it usually indicated an official concern.

"Emma Beddoes does."

"Yes, sir… George, and that's what I was hoping to talk to you about … The thing is, none of us wants to stir up hurtful memories, do we? … I've had a concern expressed that false hopes might be raised … and to be quite frank, sir, I do not see how an amateur – if you'll excuse the expression – like yourself can possibly hope to solve what an official investigation failed to resolve."

"Was it Mr Beddoes who asked you to have a word?"

"I'd rather keep that confidential ... George. I'm speaking to you out of concern for people on my patch. You're not the first ... eh non-professional to try his hand at solving this case."

"You mean Jenny Inkpen?"

"And others, sir."

"Did you have a word with them?"

"If requested at the time."

"There's no arrogance in my coming here, PC Cavendish: I'm not supposing that I have any special powers missing in the police officers who investigated Natalie's disappearance, but I do have certain advantages over someone like you.

"Which are, sir?"

"I'm not a policeman, and this has numerous advantages. Firstly, people may well feel free to tell me things they would prefer not to disclose to an official. Secondly, I'm free from the need to follow-up every possible piece of information. I can use my judgement as to whether or not it is likely to lead anywhere. I looked at the correspondence Mrs Beddoes has received and realised the vast amount of unnecessary time your people would have had to spend attempting to trace the writers – just in case they might furnish a clue. Thirdly, I'm free from the huge burden of paperwork that must be attendant on such an investigation. Fourthly, I can use my imagination to cut corners ... Do you want me to go on?"

"I don't think that will be necessary, sir. I'm glad you appreciate the nature of our task. May I ask how far you've progressed ... using your imagination?"

"Detective Chief Inspector Brockie told me that the art of investigation is to explore possibilities, confirm the negatives and eliminate all explanations of what might have happened until only one remains."

"That's very true ... George."

Bingham noticed Dave Cavendish's return to the familiar mode and smiled to himself. He'd always found that a mixture of praise and humility smoothed over many a difficult situation; and he now had an ally.

"I also understand," he continued, "that the art of police work begins with the three key elements of an investigation: motive, means and opportunity. Am I correct?"

"Yes, sir."

"I'm judging the motive in this to be as vile as any criminal act; in my opinion, more so than most, if not all. The opportunity must have sprung from mere chance: no one could have known previous to the moment it happened that Natalie would have been in that place at that time.

And so we come to means. The abductor must have had the means to snatch the child away quickly – so quickly as to be unbelievable.

We're looking for someone with a vehicle or perhaps someone on horseback. If this someone was a holiday-maker, we've missed our chance; but if it was someone from the village or someone who just happened to be in the village at that time or someone who was – and, maybe, still is – a regular visitor to the village then we might just turn up that vital lead.

I know the officers on the original investigation tried to trace any vehicles that might have been involved. Were there any unaccounted for? I don't have the files."

"We could take a look, Mr Bingham, I'm sure. I'll get in touch with John Russell, who was the village officer at the time. He still lives in Easleton. He bought the old police house when they closed the station down."

Bingham took the proffered hand and shook it warmly when Dave Cavendish rose to leave. Bingham watched him go, and noticed the spring in his step. He wondered what information John Russell might possess and what leads might lay dormant in the mind of a village bobby who would have known everyone on his patch and everything about them.

"Here we are, Mr Bingham. I didn't like to disturb you while you were talking."

Lewis Paulton placed the reed cutter's platter in front of Bingham, and Bingham was pleased to be eating it in the open air. He asked the landlord to bring him another, different, half and tucked into his lunch, while Pippa watched.

The invasion of the garden was beginning as tourists took over the seats. Bingham rather resented this, although he was aware of his own selfishness in doing so; one of the joys of retirement for him was peace and quiet. Among those arriving for lunch, he noticed Jenny Inkpen, dressed more casually than when he'd first seen her in baggy jeans and a tie-dyed top. With her was another woman unknown to Bingham: blonde, full-faced with high cheekbones. Jenny Inkpen smiled and gave him a little wave, which Bingham acknowledged.

Acknowledgement was one thing, but having his lunch interrupted quite another, and Bingham was annoyed when the two women strolled over.

"May we join you, Mr Bingham?"

Always gracious, Bingham waved a hand towards the empty places at his table, just as Lewis Paulton arrived with a half of Adnams Bitter.

"You're a half-pint man, Mr Bingham?" said Jenny Inkpen.

"It gives me a wider range on a shrinking stomach."

"Ah, Mr Bingham, you've met Ms Inkpen and one of our villagers, Mrs Hewett."

"We hadn't actually introduced ourselves, Lewis, but thank you for doing so," replied the woman Paulton had referred to as a "dyke".

"Mr Bingham's here to solve the Beddoes case."

"And are you having any luck, Mr Bingham?"

"Early days. I understand you're a writer. Fact or fiction?"

"Criminal cases. I'm probably best described as an investigative journalist."

"You've not read Jenny's *Passionate Killer*, Mr Bingham?" asked Gaye Hewett, "or *The Rapist of Lyon* or *Wild Hills, Wild Hearts*, or ..."

"That's enough, Gaye; you're teasing Mr Bingham with a plate of cakes he's never been tempted to taste. What are your theories regarding the disappearance of Natalie Beddoes, Mr Bingham? May I call you ... we've never been told your first name."

"George," replied Bingham, reluctantly, since he had no wish to be on first name terms with either woman.

"I'm Jenny and this is Gaye. So what are your theories, George?"

"I don't have any."

"Really!" exclaimed Gaye Hewett, "We thought you were a detective."

"Then you thought like Cox's pig, and he thought wrong."

"Cox's pig?" queried Jenny Inkpen.

"It's a Midland's expression," replied Bingham, "He wasn't expecting to end up in the slaughterhouse."

Bingham noticed the women exchanged glances, eyebrows raised and a quizzical smile on their lips, and he was pleased they thought themselves to be talking to a buffoon.

"As a writer, I could postulate a number of explanations."

Bingham was sure she could, but had rather hoped she wouldn't.

"May I get you a drink?" he asked.

"Umm, yes, oh thank you. A g and t for me and – Gaye?"

"The same – thank you."

Bingham nodded to Paulton and the landlord left to fetch the drinks.

"From the beginning, the police concentrated on the assumption that Natalie had been abducted," continued Jenny, "but another possibility is that she was murdered. Who were the last people to see her alive – her mother and, possibly, her grandmother.

Her father was supposed to be on the harvest field, but was he? The farmer took a while to find him. Where was he during the missing hour and a half?

She and her sister had a row that morning. Where were the sister and her boyfriend during that time?"

"Moira was eight years old and the current boyfriend about eleven I would say – having only met him once … "

"Child murderers are not unknown, George. Mary Bell? Thompson and Venables? I believe, if you do your research, you'll find that they were all less than eleven years old when they killed another child."

"I see no evidence to suggest any such thing."

"You do know that children are sexually aware at a very early age, George, don't you? Or are you with the generation that believes in the innocence of childhood?"

"I don't think you should suppose that children lack innocence because they express curiosity."

"But you can't dismiss the fact that she may have been murdered," said Gaye Hewett, "End of."

"End of?"

"I think we'd better leave George to enjoy his lunch in peace, Gaye," suggested Jenny Inkpen, as she rose from her seat at the table, "If ever you want to discuss the case, George, come round and see me sometime. I live on what the locals call the 'top road'."

"Yes, I know. I saw your house last night."

For a moment but only for a moment, Bingham saw a look of surprise cross Jenny Inkpen's face; and then she, her friend and the look had moved away to their original table where they'd left their coats.

Bingham turned to his cheese platter, disturbed. He was conscious of having been off-hand with the two women and of having disliked them both but couldn't put his finger on precisely why this was so. In part, it was the 'half-pint' comment that carried a sneer in its tone; in part, it was Jenny Inkpen's use of the term 'investigative journalist' to describe herself when the titles of her books suggested that she merely sensationalised violent crime; in part, it was Gaye Hewett's comment 'we thought you were a detective'; in part, it was the knowing looks that were exchanged on several occasions by the women as though they and they alone held the secrets of the universe; in part, it was their free theorising that paid no regard for the people involved; in part, it was the way they had left their coats, reserving one table while sitting at another. However, the parts didn't amount to a whole and Bingham was ashamed of himself, but only slightly.

He was tired. He always was after lunch and the intense heat of midday only intensified this feeling; the idea of a doze seemed even more attractive than it had an hour ago. In his room, Bingham removed his shoes and jacket, but stretched out on the bed with the rest of his clothes still on.

When he woke, sweat running uncomfortably from his neck into the collar of his shirt the day had moved on; his watch said three-thirty, and Bingham realised he'd slept for over two hours. Perhaps he should be at home; Lina would be bringing him a cup of tea, now, with a slice of one of her cakes. Perhaps, at seventy-one, he was too old for detective work; those annoying women might have been right.

"A cup of tea, Mr Bingham?"

"That sounds marvellous, Mrs Paulton," he replied, entering the bar.

"I have some Suffolk scones. "

"Even more so."

He sat in the window, watched the road and thought of Emma Beddoes while he enjoyed the tea and scones. It had been Lina's mother who introduced him to Suffolk scones; they hadn't been part of his childhood in Wolverhampton, where pikelets graced his childhood teatimes. Pikelets were called crumpets in Suffolk.

As he'd grown older, Bingham had become more conscious than ever of the importance of words, of phrases, of expressions. Always a listener, his natural ability had sharpened with age. 'Someone somewhere knew …', and it had to be someone in the village. He was sure of that fact. It was a fact; it couldn't be otherwise. Unless … yes, unless it was a tourist, long gone.

A minibus passed by the window, and pulled up opposite The Smack, scattering the dry dust into the air. Several children scrambled out and look around, their faces red with the heat.

"That'll be the school bus, Mr Bingham. There's only a handful go from here to Middleham and the bus drops them off about teatime every day. That'll be Mrs Peck after her boy."

"Mrs Peck?" queried Bingham, the name ringing a bell.

"Her as was Olive Freeman. She married Mike Peck. He works in Leiston."

"The courting couple who saw and heard nothing?"

"That's right. Mind you, who could wonder at that!" replied the landlady, laughing, "Would you like to speak to her?"

"Yes please."

"I'll have a word."

Teresa Paulton's 'word' brought Bingham to the Peck's house early in the evening.

"We've put David to bed," said Mike Peck as he opened the door to Bingham, "We thought it might be quieter that way."

"How old is your son?"

"Only four. He goes to the afternoon nursery," replied Olive Peck.

"You started early," laughed Bingham, nodding at Olive Peck who was showing signs of her second child.

She blushed and threw a look at her husband, as though she expected him to defend her against Bingham's remark.

"My wife and I were late starters," said Bingham, aware of the offence he might have caused, "I was in my early forties and my wife in her late thirties, but we managed to have four children."

"You didn't waste any time then," laughed Mike Peck.

"No."

Bingham's 'confession' relaxed the atmosphere and the Pecks invited him to sit. Their sitting room was furnished ornately in the country cottage style: two light, wooden chairs and a matching settee with floral cushions and throws, a rug covering the floorboards, a folding table secreted under the small, latticed window, brasses, flowers and beams. Bingham smiled. It was simple but tasteful, and within their budget.

"You wanted to ask us about Natalie," said Mike Peck, as Olive went for the inevitable pot of tea.

"If you don't mind. It struck me as odd that you heard nothing."

"What do you mean?"

"I took a look at the field and it curves up towards the very spot where Natalie disappeared. I can understand you seeing nothing but I can't understand you hearing nothing, if you were at that end of the field at that time, and I assume you were – away from the farm and the gate?"

"We told the truth," insisted Olive Peck from the doorway into the kitchen.

"Did you – the whole truth?"

"We didn't see anything."

"Maybe not, but you heard something, didn't you? A courting couple would have had one ear on the road and the farm."

"I think you'd better go, Mr Bingham. My wife and I don't like being called liars, and you've no business asking us questions anyway."

"You're quite right, and I will go if you insist, but this may be your chance to put the record straight, to clear your consciences."

The desire to confess was a strong one in decent people, thought Bingham. His dealings with children guilty of no more than misdemeanours had convinced him of this fact; and now he watched the Pecks as the foundations of their secure little world were shaken if only slightly.

"We didn't see what happened to Natalie. It was only later that we remembered …"

"And you didn't think it was that important and you didn't want to get involved too deeply?"

"My mum and dad would have gone mad," said Olive.

"How old were you?"

"Fourteen."

"They didn't know we were in Tony Ship's field that day," said Mike, "and so we told the police that we hadn't seen or heard anything. If we'd have seen what happened, we'd have said."

"What did you hear?"

"A car or something, but we didn't realise 'til later."

"You're sure it was a car?"

"It might have been a van. There was lots of traffic about, coming and going to the beach. We didn't rate it as important."

"In which direction did this car or van go?"

"It went down to the beach."

"We're not sure it was to the beach. It might have been to Easleton," said Olive.

"If it was into the village, which road did it take?"

"Down towards the vicarage – we think."

"Did you hear or see it pass the gate into Ship's field?"

"No! I swear we saw nothing."

"It's true, Mr Bingham, "Mike's telling the truth."

Chapter Five

'WHEN SHALL WE THREE MEET AGAIN?'

Bingham wasn't inclined to suspect the Peck's of anything other than self-interest. After all, what young couple involved in a bit of how's-your-father would want their parents to find out? If what you knew didn't seem important it was best to keep quiet.

Nevertheless, they had withheld information that might have given the police a vital clue. Bingham couldn't help but wonder whether this applied to anyone else.

He left the Peck's small cottage and made his way along the main street of Aldewich, Pippa lolloping along by his side, now quite used to the terrain and her master's wanderings within it. More by accident than design, Bingham found himself walking past Percy's and onto the beach. He recalled his conversation with Amos.

"They were looking everywhere but never in the right place. I'm saying no more."

Did he mean anything by that remark or was he just pretending to know something?

Bingham was a townsman himself, unused to the sea and its vagaries but he liked the sound of the waves breaking gently along the shoreline. The unbearable heat of the day was subsiding, replaced by a cool onshore breeze and with it a slight sea mist. Near the shore's edge he found a stone and skimmed it across the still water.

Nine bounces were all he achieved; as a child, on a seaside holiday, Bingham had managed sixteen. He felt thirsty and hungry, but considered it too early for his evening meal.

He took his mobile phone from his pocket. Lina answered the call.

"I'm sorry ... I meant to phone you this morning ... No, I didn't forget exactly. Are the animals all right? Has Phil fed the bees? ... No, well yes, I am getting somewhere but I'm not sure where. ... I haven't eaten since lunch. ... No, I shan't neglect Pippa. I fed her before I went out ... to see a young couple ... No, I don't think so ..."

Lina's questions were beginning to weary him, but he was glad he'd phoned and it was good to hear her voice again. When she'd finished talking, he left the beach and made his way back to the bend in the road. A short stroll before dinner seemed a good idea: along the road past the monastery or along the clifftop. Bingham wasn't sure. He wanted to avoid Natalie's footpath. It was quiet after a hectic day – the tourists had gone home – and the road was safe for Pippa, but Bingham decided to take the cliff path.

He paused at the gate where he'd met Moira and her boyfriend, dropped into a small gulley and found a track through the wood. Passing a rear entrance to the monastery grounds, he wondered how he might approach the staff. He had no authority to ask questions. So far he'd been lucky: people had come to him. Perhaps he'd just stroll in and wait to be accosted.

Eventually, the trail led him by the Beddoes house and onto the 'even more private road' where three women stood gossiping. He knew this by the intensity of their manner and the way in which they leaned towards each other absorbed in the conversation. Two of them he had already met – Jenny Inkpen and Gaye Hewitt – but the third woman was new to him. It was only the fact that she was astride a horse that made Bingham assume her to be Mavis Tilt, who had been out riding with her husband the day Natalie disappeared. She was a type once described as buxom: big firm breasts, big firm hips and thighs like barrels. Bingham had no doubt the horse was held firmly in her grip, as she leaned over its neck the better to hear what Jenny Inkpen was saying.

Bingham, always inconspicuous whenever he entered a room, was almost up to the women before they saw him. When they did, all three look startled and greeted him with hard stares. They looked so much like conspirators that Bingham was reminded of the three witches hailing Macbeth. He couldn't help imagining what they might have been brewing.

Mavis Tilt was the first to recover her composure and turned her horse towards him. It was a threatening move: the large stallion bore down upon him and Bingham stepped aside.

"He won't tread on you, Mr Bingham. I have him under control. I'm Mavis Tilt. I understand you're looking for Natalie Beddoes. Good luck. Many have been called to the task, but none chosen to succeed."

She leaned down and shook Bingham's hand. It was a solid, manly handshake, which matched her chipped and cheery tone.

"If you'll excuse me, I must go. My husband will have our dinner cooked to perfection within half-an-hour and I have to rub Reggie down. He sweats like a Turkish wrestler's jock strap in this heat. Let's hope the weather breaks. We could do with a drop of rain; it keeps the holidaymakers away."

With a hearty laugh and a wave of her riding crop to the other two, Mavis Tilt urged Reggie into a trot and disappeared from view.

"You have us all talking, George," said Jenny Inkpen, "Have you come to hear my scenarios?"

"I was walking Pippa, but I'd be pleased to listen."

"Then let me invite you for lunch tomorrow. Shall we say noon? I like to eat early. We can swop theories all afternoon."

"I'd be delighted to come. Thank you."

"I must be going, Jenny," said Gaye Hewitt, "Joe will be wondering where I am. He hasn't had his tea yet."

"I'm on my way to The Smack. Perhaps we could walk together?"

"Um, yes, of course, but I don't have much to tell you, Mr Bingham."

"You don't have to tell me anything."

With a wave, Jenny Inkpen disappeared behind her beech hedge and Bingham dropped into step alongside Gaye Hewitt, who seemed silent and uncomfortable.

"Your son, Joseph, was six or seven at the time, wasn't he?" asked Bingham.

"Yes."

"I suppose you must have a great deal of sympathy for Mr and Mrs Beddoes."

"Do you?"

"I haven't spoken to Mr Beddoes, but after meeting with Natalie's mother my heart went out to her."

"Why?" asked Gaye Hewitt.

"That seems a strange question to me."

"Natalie's disappearance is clearly their fault."

"I don't see why."

"A child's safety is the parents' responsibility."

The smugness of the answer didn't surprise Bingham. He'd come across similar attitudes to other situations in women of Gave Hewitt's generation – the thirty-somethings who had a sure answer to all life's problems, a slick answer garnered from last month's women's magazines and shared by everyone in their circle.

"I can imagine letting my daughters ride their bikes to their nana's without thinking they might be abducted."

Bingham noticed Gaye Hewitt stiffen with disapproval. His instinctive dislike of her was beginning to harden.

"You consider Emma Beddoes to be negligent?"

"It's the parents who are responsible for their children's safety."

"Have you spoken with Emma Beddoes?"

"Our paths don't cross very often."

"What do you remember about the day Natalie disappeared?"

"Nothing much, to be honest. We'd just finished our lunch and I was clearing away the dishes. I didn't hear what was going on outside until the police came knocking."

"That would be John Russell?"

"Yes. He took over the search before the main police and detectives turned up."

"I understand there was a service for Natalie on the Sunday following her disappearance. Did you attend?"

"No."

"May I ask why?"

"I don't believe in that sort of thing. I don't think it helps."

"How did your son, Joseph, react to his school friend's disappearance?"

"They weren't really friends. They never played together."

"He never mentioned Natalie's disappearance?"

"He might have done. I don't remember. He's a quiet boy. He doesn't say much."

"You've never had any thoughts yourself about what happened?"

"We were all frightened at the time, but life goes on."

"Did you take any extra precautions with Joseph?"

"No more than usual. I always walk him to the school bus stop or to his friend's, if he plays out. If Mrs Beddoes had done the same, her daughter might be here today."

"Do many of the villagers feel like you about Mr and Mrs Beddoes?"

"I wouldn't know."

"How about Mrs Tilt?"

"You'd be better off asking her."

"I will. Does your son go riding?"

"I don't see what that's got to do with anything."

"Perhaps it hasn't ... The Tilt's run a riding school, don't they?"

"Yes, they have an old farmhouse near Easleton."

"But they live near Ms Inkpen?"

"Yes. Their daughter runs the riding school and lives in the farmhouse."

"Is that where her husband was cooking their dinner this evening?"

"I imagine so, since she rode off in that direction."

By now they had reached the spot where Natalie's bicycle had fallen, and Bingham stopped dead. Gaye

Hewitt turned to him and followed his eyes to the ground.

"Are you sure you're not a detective?"

"Yes. Why do you ask?"

"You've questioned me more intensely than the police did. You're not a private detective, are you?"

"No. I imagine they had more people to question, more paperwork to process and mile after mile of heath and woodland to search. Is the Tilt's riding school remote? Is it beyond Easleton Heath?"

"It's this side of the Easleton to Aldewich road just beyond our stretch of heathland. Now, if you don't mind, I'd like to get my son's tea."

Bingham watched her walk towards the six foot solid wooden gates that shielded her bungalow from the road.

"Do you socialise with the Tilts?"

"I beg your pardon."

"Do you and Ms Inkpen mix socially with the Tilts?"

"I really don't see what that's got to do with you, Mr Bingham. End of."

With this final parry, Gaye Hewitt disappeared behind her gates, leaving Bingham pondering on the phrase that seemed to be a favourite of hers.

There had been other questions he wanted to ask; the social dynamics of this little Suffolk village were emerging and he wanted to understand their significance. There were the farmers and the fishermen, the holidaymakers who came and went, those – like the Peck's – who had been born in the village but now found employment elsewhere, those who provided a kind of social cohesion such as the church and the pub but may or may not have felt a natural loyalty to the village; and then there were the newcomers – those whose money enabled them to buy up derelict properties as second homes or permanent residences.

In the middle of this flux of humanity was little Natalie Beddoes, who had disappeared six years ago, gone but not forgotten.

Bingham stood watching the gravel patch at the end of Gwen Davis's driveway for a long time. It seemed odd that this was the last place on earth where the child's presence could be felt here in Aldewich. He saw the fallen cycle and the spinning wheel, and looked up and down the three roads that led off from the fork: to Easleton, to the church and to the beach.

His daughter, Cecilia, had a nine-year-old son who was bound to have a bike; Bingham felt for his mobile phone and rang his daughter who lived in London.

"Hello, Cecilia, this is dad ... yes, I'm fine, thanks. Will you do me a favour? ... Your mum's fine ... No, there's nothing to worry about ... The dogs are all right ... yes and the cats ... There's nothing wrong. Bruno does have a bike, doesn't he? Would you get him to spin the back wheel for me, place the bike on the ground and time how long the wheel takes to stop spinning? ... I'll tell you later ... I know it's dinner time ... Tomorrow will do or at the weekend ...Yes, thank you, darling. Love to Bruno."

Bingham's two daughters were twins and named by his wife Cecilia and Fiorenza after two Italian opera singers she admired. To date, Bruno was his only grandchild, born 'out of wedlock', as they used to say when Bingham was a boy. Thank God we now have 'single parents' rather than 'unmarried mothers', he thought and his mind went back to his conversation with Gaye Hewett. No father had been mentioned.

It was time for dinner, and his old appetite had been sharpened by the walk.

"We've a nice home-glazed Blytham ham, Mr Bingham," said Teresa Paulton, showing him to a seat in the near corner of the bar, "with local free range eggs, handmade chunky chips and homemade pineapple relish.

"I'll skip the ham and have an extra egg, Mrs Paulton, and a half of the Adnams Bitter and Cliff Quay's Tolly Roger. Oh and ..."

"... a bowl of water for Pippa. Are you a vegetarian, then, Mr Bingham?"

"Yes."

"You look well on it, I must say."

"And the pigs feel that much the better, Mrs Paulton."

Bingham's entrance had caused a similar stir in the bar to the one he'd created on his arrival. Was that only yesterday? He seemed to have been in Aldewich for ages. Amos Pritchard sat with the carter, Tony Ship, and Natalie's father. Bingham realized he'd only actually spoken to one of them for any length of time. They all glared at him and Alan Beddoes stood as if to leave, only to be restrained by the carter's rough hand, which he shook off. He crossed the room to Bingham's table and scowled down at him.

"Mr Bingham, I think we need to talk."

"Shall we go outside?"

"Not now. We're in the middle of a game."

"Can I buy you a drink?"

"I have to be in the right frame of mind. Later."

Curtness seemed to be the order of the day thought Bingham, as Alan Beddoes returned to his friends.

After he'd eaten, Bingham strolled into the garden with a half pint in each hand, hoping Alan Beddoes might seek him, but after fifteen minutes or so there was no sign of Natalie's father. He wondered whether or not to phone Lina, but decided to wait until he retired for the night. She was often late to bed and he might catch her anytime up until midnight. For a second time since he'd arrived in Aldewich, Bingham wished he was home chatting to his wife across the width of the fireplace with their dogs between them on the tufted rug.

He wondered why he'd asked Gaye Hewitt about the Tilt's riding school. He was aware his questions lacked order and coherence. He was building a detailed picture of Aldewich as it might have been on the afternoon Natalie disappeared, but none of the pathways he now had in mind led anywhere: round and round in circles, and always back to the patch of gravel at the end of Gwen Davis's driveway.

It was a question of speed; whoever had snatched Natalie had whisked her away in a moment of time. Bingham's thinking returned to the Tilt's farmhouse and stables. Was the little girl buried somewhere less than a few miles away?

"Mr Bingham?"

He looked up at the speaker, a fresh-faced young man with blond hair, blue eyes and an intense stare. His manner, one of attention and service, told Bingham that this was John Russell, the policeman who had looked after the villages six years ago.

"Thanks for coming. PC Cavendish said he'd contact you promptly."

"You asked for details of any vehicles that warranted our attention on the day Natalie Beddoes disappeared?

"Yes."

"May I sit down?"

"Please. Let me get you a drink. You're not actually on duty, are you?"

"No, I'll have a Guinness if you don't mind."

"I'd mind much more if you didn't, although why you want to drink Guinness when the local beers are so excellent beats me."

John Russell looked perplexed at Bingham's remark, smiled and opened a wallet folder he pulled from under his arm. By the time Bingham returned with the Guinness and another half pint, this time of Adnams Bitter, the policeman had spread his papers across the table.

"You understand that my giving you this information is off the record, don't you, Mr Bingham? It's only because Dave Cavendish mentioned that you were a friend of DCI Simon Brockie that I'm even thinking of doing this. He was a good man. He returned here time and time again, long after the case was offering no new leads. He was a good friend to the Beddoes and much admired in the village."

"Did you check with him?"

"No. PC Cavendish's word was good enough for me. Besides, in my job you get used to summing people up quickly and I can see you're the right sort."

Bingham had always been considered 'the right sort' by all who knew him, even those with whom he'd crossed swords. He'd never understood why, but the knowledge was a comfort.

"It was impossible to account for every car that had been in the village that day. Percy's restaurant served over two hundred meals, and not everyone who visited the beach would have eaten there. The Smack served a hundred and twenty-one lunches and other people would have brought picnics. There might have been in excess of five hundred visitors to Aldewich over the course of the day and most would have come in cars.

We put out a request for information and two hundred people came forward. Technically, you might say we had over three hundred suspects among the visitors alone – those who didn't come forward."

"Were there any means of transport – excuse the expression, but we need to think further than cars and vans – that were sighted on the move in the vicinity between about 1.30 when Natalie left home and 1.39 when Emma Beddoes rang you?"

"There was the white Ford Fiesta who passed Gwen Davis's driveway after Natalie disappeared. The couple came forward and reported seeing Natalie's bike propped against the fence but nothing else."

"How far from the scene were the Tilt's riding?"

"They were on Easleton Heath about a mile away."

"And could have covered the distance in a couple of minutes? Were the stables searched?"

"As a matter of routine, all buildings were searched."

"Where was Tony Ship?"

"His truck was thoroughly examined by the forensic boys and girls – much to his disgust."

"But where was he?"

"He was carting some rubble from Eastwold to a local tip. We checked with the builders who hired him."

"Are there any other locals who might have been on the move at that time?"

"There was Ian Marjoram, who clears gardens and that kind of thing. He also supplies logs and kindling. The Forestry Commission uses his services at times, and so timber comes his way, you might say. He was working in Aldewich Forest."

"But no other locals?"

"No. You seem to think this was a local matter, Mr Bingham."

"I don't think anything, John – and call me George. There were a number of sightings reported. Were any vehicles involved in those?"

"There was a grey van in Eastwold that was never traced, but no one in the village recalled seeing it. It's disheartening, isn't it, George – so much time and effort and nothing to show for it. One villain defeats the efforts of an entire police force."

"There may have been more than one person involved, mightn't there? You don't like to think of it being one of your locals, do you, John?"

"No, I don't. I accept it could be, but my money's on a holidaymaker who just happened to be driving home at the precise moment Natalie appeared at the end of that footpath."

The two men sat in silence for a while, John Russell refusing the offer of a second Guinness on the grounds that he was driving. They shook hands when he left and Bingham accompanied him to his car before heading off along the main street with Pippa on her final walk of the day.

The police officer had hit at least one nail squarely on the head when he referred to the 'precise moment'. Time and again, Bingham came across the word 'chance' in his thinking.

He saw no reason to suppose that the culprit was likely to be a holidaymaker any more than a local. Such alibis as existed were loose ones: the Tilts spoke for each other, Tony Ship might have been anywhere on the road, Marjoram – a name new to Bingham – might have been in the forest. The crime had occurred in that sleepy hour after lunch when some were still at their meal and others were dozing.

It was a question of sightings, familiarity and timing. It was impossible to rely on any of these factors. Who could really be sure that anyone was where they said they were at any particular time? When you're used to seeing people going about their daily business in familiar places, after a while you don't pay much attention. One meeting might be mixed up with another; an incident that took place one day might be placed forty-eight hours later. It wasn't a question of honesty; it was a matter of custom.

"George!"

The hearty voice of John Crisp roused Bingham from his reverie, and he rather resented the disturbance to his thoughts.

"Good evening," he replied, politely.

"Are we getting anywhere?"

"I don't know."

"It's early days."

Bingham was puzzled as to why priests felt obliged to look on the bright side: six years after a child had disappeared could hardly be looked upon as 'early days'. But he mustn't judge the man: after all, he had placed flowers and said prayers for Natalie every week for those six years.

"I met three of your parishioners earlier today deep in conversation – Mavis Tilt, Gaye Hewitt… "

"… and Jenny Inkpen?

"What's the connection between them?"

"Jenny represents London and the Arts – with a capital 'A' – for both other women. She dresses the part, she acts the part and to all intents and purposes she is the part. When her London friends come down for a weekend, Mavis Tilt and Gaye are invited."

"Did they know each other before she moved down here which was, I believe, after Natalie disappeared?"

"Not as far as I know. The Tilts have had their second home here for years and I never saw Jenny at any of their dos. It's an area that attracts Londoners. We have the Aldeburgh Festival just down the road."

Bingham liked Benjamin Britten's work. He and Lina went to several events every year. His mind wandered off across the salt marshes and he saw reed warblers flitting about in the sunlight. Recalled to Aldewich, he asked:

"And Gaye Hewitt?"

"Gaye's a local girl – a trained midwife, actually. She was born in Leiston and moved here just after I arrived, which would be a little over seven years ago."

"Not long before her son was born?"

"Yes."

"Has there ever been any sign of a father?"

"No. I know nothing about that side of her life."

"Does the boy come to Sunday School?"

"Yes. Most of the village children do. It gives their parents a little time to themselves. Besides, there's more to the church than mere Christianity in a place like Aldewich."

The evening had closed in by the time the two men reached the gate of the vicarage. Gnats were dancing in the last light of the long, summer day; it promised to be another hot one on the morrow. Bingham poked a finger inside his shirt collar and relieved the pressure on his neck, wiping away the sweat as he did so. Lights were going on in the house, and Bingham could see Eileen

Crisp moving about and drawing the curtains against any insects that might be tempted to intrude.

He thought of Lina doing much the same back home at Bob's Farm. He wondered how their other two dogs were faring and pictured the cats getting ready to go out for the night. Had he phoned Lina today? He couldn't remember. Not for the second or even third time since he arrived, Bingham wondered what he was doing in Aldewich.

"Do you mind if I borrow your bike for a short while tomorrow morning," he asked John Crisp.

Chapter Six
LIFE GOES ON

Bingham felt uncomfortable borrowing the vicar's bike: mainly because of what it implied for Pippa. Both he and Lina despised people who exercised their dogs while cycling themselves: the dog was forced to keep up a certain pace and had no chance to experience the joys of sniffing their way along a trail. He had the choice of leaving her at The Smack, but knew she would object to being parted from his company, especially in a strange place. At the same time, he wanted to time Alan Beddoes' route to and from work and to do this he must cycle; besides, if Alan Beddoes had anything to say 'it was better out than in' – a philosophy Bingham had inherited from his mother, but with which he didn't fully agree.

Teresa Paulton had been a mine of information regarding Natalie's father's route and soon after breakfast, when he was served Welsh rabbit at his own request, Bingham was making his way by Gaye Hewitt's gates towards the spot where Natalie disappeared. Pippa, having refused to stay behind, trotted along at his side.

"One word to Lina," he said to the Labrador, "and we part company."

Pippa looked up at him and seemed to smile: she had a large mouth that curled up at the ends.

Teresa Paulton had said Alan Beddoes would cycle from his cottage along the private road that reached the Aldewich – Easleton road above the place of his daughter's disappearance and, after a short distance, reach a footpath and bridleway that crossed by several fields, taking him directly to the farm where he worked. Bingham's intention was to be on the bridleway ahead of him, and he was waiting when Alan Beddoes arrived.

"I can't stop now."

"There's no need: we can ride together," replied Bingham.

He nodded to Pippa who fell in behind the two men as they cycled side by side along the narrow, grass-rucked track

"I've nothing against you as a man, Mr Bingham. I'm sure you know what you're up to, but your questioning is upsetting Emma and the household."

"Your wife asked to see me, Mr Beddoes."

"It's false hopes, Mr Bingham. You're offering her false hopes. Stirring up the dust of the past that's best left to settle. There's no way that we're going to find our little girl now. You know that, I know that and, in her heart, Emma knows that but won't admit it. Some things are best left alone and this is one of them."

"Why the reluctance to find your daughter, Mr Beddoes?"

Alan Beddoes bike screeched to a halt as he braked, and he tipped to one side, almost collapsing into the hedge. He looked away from Bingham, down at the ground, adjusting the canvas satchel, which held his lunch and was strapped to a carrier on the back of the cycle. Bingham's brutal question had anticipated the tears in his eyes.

"People think I have no feelings. I know that, but I can't go on hoping against hope that we'll see her little face again. And what I fear most is that we will find her … or what's left of her … buried somewhere out there in the forest or on that blasted heath. Do I want that, Mr Bingham? Does Emma really want that?

"My old spark has gone from me, and the only way I can cope is to get on with things, get on with my life, do my job. Emma was upset at first but she understands me better now. I've got to be doing something or I'll burst."

Alan Beddoes hadn't looked up, while delivering what Bingham assumed was a long speech.

"At first, she thought I wasn't grieving. She thought it wrong that I went back to work so early but there was no other way. I've tried to be a good husband, I've tried to comfort Emma but it isn't in my nature to be … to be …"

"Demonstrative?"

Alan Beddoes looked up at Bingham, no longer – it seemed – ashamed of the tears in his eyes.

"You're not like the others, are you?" he said, "Emma said that. He's different, she said."

"Your wife is consumed by her grief, Mr Beddoes. She'll find no peace until she knows, however terrible the knowing."

"Natalie is in her head all the time, and she resents me being able to get away from it. I don't think Emma's cooked a meal, made a bed, done the washing or watched television but she's seen Natalie somewhere in what she was doing. But it isn't helping find Natalie, is it?"

"When do you think of your child? What's your abiding memory of her?"

"I think of her looking up and seeing a stranger's face looking down on her. If ever I came across the man, Mr Bingham, I would kill him. Against all I hold right and holy I'd kill him."

"You're convinced it was a man?"

"Would a woman do such a thing?"

"It has been known."

"I want to help, Mr Bingham. I want to do the right thing, but I can't help you. I was on the harvest field that day until the gaffer came with Emma's message, and then I cycled home as fast as I could. I swear to God it's true. I've thought and thought but I know nothing."

"Have you anything to do with the people at the monastery?"

"Why, you don't think they're involved?"

"I don't think anything, Mr Beddoes. I'm just trying to place where people were during those few minutes of that day."

"I saw no one about on my way back. I did look in the field where Mrs Tilt keeps her horses but there was no one there. You're like me, aren't you Mr Bingham, you think Natalie's to be found somewhere in the village, don't you?"

"I have no idea, Mr Beddoes."

Bingham watched as Alan Beddoes looked up and down the lane; he could see that the man had talked himself round and needed to be on his way. He saw him brush the back of one hand across his face, obviously embarrassed by an inappropriate sense of urgency.

"I must be on my way. I'll be late."

"I know."

"If you think of anything, Mr Bingham, I'll be only too pleased to talk again."

"Thank you."

Alan Beddoes offered a clumsy hand, which Bingham held and shook, and then the farm labourer was off down the lane. Bingham looked after him for a while, finally turning back the way he had come. Somehow he didn't feel the need to time his journey anymore. A policeman would have done so, of course, if only to eliminate the possibility. 'Confirm the negatives': Bingham could hear his friend Brockie's voice as he reached the road.

It was still early morning, and Bingham was at a loose end. Until now people had come to him. Where should he go from here? He wheeled the bike with Pippa at his side, strangely relieved that he hadn't made her run alongside too far. He stopped at the gate he'd climbed on his first day – the gate into the young lovers' field – and waited. Perhaps Tony Ship would appear and say something that might offer a move forward? There was no sound from the derelict farmyard. Perhaps the carter was already at work? Did someone mention a wife? Bingham thought so, but couldn't be sure. He listened for the sound of any movement – perhaps washing being hung out? He heard nothing.

Further along the road, as he approached the vicarage, Bingham saw wild briar roses and elder in bloom. If any flowers did, those two spoke of midsummer and lazy days on the cricket field. Memories of the pungent smell of the elderflower took him back to his time as a boy. Butterflies flitted in and around the blossoms in the hedges. Beyond the hedge, a harvester was cutting wheat or perhaps it was barley. Soon the round hay bales would brighten the fields, golden cylinders against the dark earth. Summertime and the sweet scents of the countryside beckoned him to a lazy day. By the roadside a song thrush cracked a snail against a stone again and again before gobbling down the succulent flesh. Bingham felt himself drifting into the way of the countryside.

There was no one in at the vicarage and so Bingham propped the bike against the house wall and left quietly, making his way to Percy's café on the beach and an early coffee. He sat outside watching the empty car park: in an hour or so the tourists would arrive. He sat quietly, picturing the village and its people. The children would be gone by now, off to school, and those who worked would be at their employment, perhaps in the village, perhaps further afield.

Yesterday – no, the day before – these people had been strangers to him. On first meeting he had seen them from the outside, watching the way they moved and dressed, shook hands, smiled, the way they spoke; but now he was getting to know them, putting himself in their shoes, thinking as they did. At least one of them knew something; Bingham was convinced this was true. If this was so, how had they lived with themselves for the past six years knowing what they did?

Pippa was unusually restless: catching his mood, no doubt.

"Come on. Let's find our inspiration in walking."

She seemed to know the place better than he did and led Bingham behind the restaurant to the track that ran along the top of the cliffs. These were crumbling badly, eroded by the incessant battering of the sea. At the very edge, trees were toppling down onto the beach. Warning notices advised holidaymakers to keep clear, but still they climbed the soft sand, keen to reach the top and look down on their success.

It was close to the edge that he met for the second time the youth he'd seen with Moira Beddoes: cigarette in mouth, a scowl on his lips. The youth fondled Pippa's ears; he obviously liked dogs.

"We're shifting this tree. The conservation people asked us to do it," he explained.

"Where's your Dad?"

"We forgot the crosscut. He's gone to get it."

"Then you'll have a little time on your hands, won't you: time for a smoke and time for a chat?"

"I told you the other day. I don't know nothing."

"You may have told yourself that but you never told me. Is there somewhere we can sit?"

The youth looked at Bingham as he might have looked at his grandfather asking for a hand down the church steps. He grinned and took Bingham's arm.

"There's a seat by the clifftop, but we'll have to be careful. There's a lot of subsidence here."

The seat was on the very edge of the crumbling cliff. Bingham looked down. He had no heads for heights, but at the very least he thought he would fall into soft sand.

"Mind your dog don't fall over the edge," the youth remarked with a grin.

Once they were seated, he took a packet of cigarettes from his pocket, flicked one into his mouth, struck a match and cupped the flame in his hands. He was cool now. Bingham could see the tension drain from him.

"Are you Moira's boyfriend?"

"Yeah, sort of."

"What's your name?"

"Pete, Pete Marjoram," replied the youth after a moment's hesitation.

"And you'll be ... 17?"

"Yeah," he replied, obviously impressed at Bingham's perspicacity.

"Where were you the day Natalie disappeared?"

"I was only 11! I didn't have nothing to do with it!"

"I didn't say you did. Where were you?"

"I was playing on the beach.

"By yourself?"

"In the end. I'd been with Joe Hewitt. We were playing in the pub yard and then we went down to the beach."

"Just the two of you?"

"Yeah ... No, the landlord's kid came down with us, but then they went back and I stayed down there. They were younger than me, but there ain't many kids to play with in the village."

"And now you work with your Dad?"

"Yeah. We do odd jobs, help out at the harvest and we supply logs and kindling. I can bring you a buck of logs any time you want."

"What do you make of Natalie's disappearance?"

"I told you, I had nothing to do with it."

"But you must have thought about it, and you must have heard people speculate."

"It's a big forest out there and a big heath. It'd be easy to bury someone and they'd never be found."

"I thought the police had searched the area thoroughly with dogs and helicopters."

"Do you know how many derelict farm buildings there are about, full of diesel and other smells? You could hide a body for days and then get rid of it when the time was right. Besides, if you judge the tides right, you could take a boat out and drop a body overboard, anytime."

"You know the sea as well as the forest?"

"Yeah. The fishermen go out whenever there's the chance of a catch. I've been out."

"Who with?"

"What's this?"

"Just answer the question."

"Amos and one or two of the others."

"So you can handle a boat?"

"You trying to needle me or what?"

Bingham smiled. Yes, he was trying to needle the boy. It was rather like being back at work in school when he'd had to deal with a lad who'd been up to no good. Needle the truth out quickly and have done with the matter. Why call the parents and counsellors in? Why make a mountain out of a mole hill?

"Will you go before my Dad gets back? I don't want him to think I'm in trouble."

"Yes, son, I'll be on my way. Just one more thing – what do you make of Moira's grandmother?"

"She's all right. Bit sharp. She don't like me, thinks I'm too old for Moira."

"At the moment, she's right. In two or three years' time, it might be different. Remember what I said. I'll be seeing you."

Bingham was tired. His conversations with Alan Beddoes and Pete Marjoram had exhausted him; and the thought of lunch with Jenny Inkpen (what a bloody silly name!) left him completely drained. What could the woman want to say? Was he yet another sounding board for her theories? Bingham looked at his watch. It was coffee time, but he'd had his coffee and it was too early for a pre-lunch beer. Besides, he could hardly turn up at a lady's house smelling of alcohol.

He hadn't spoken to Natalie's grandmother, Gwen Davies, as yet. He didn't like to remind her of that tragic day, and doubted she could tell him anything that might point the way. But if she was like her daughter, Emma Beddoes, Gwen Davies would expect a visit. Bingham strolled that way.

He felt directionless. A police officer would have a purpose; their questions would have been considered and discussed before they left the station. They'd know what they were attempting to clarify. In the same thought, he realised he wasn't being fair on himself: in his mind, Bingham knew he had as complete a picture as anyone of the village on that afternoon six years ago.

He came, unexpectedly, out on to the private road that led past the Beddoes house. There it was before him, and to his right was the footpath: the one he'd hesitated to walk. Bingham wasn't superstitious as regards cats and ladders, but he had a sense of everything in its time: that to anticipate an answer before the facts were clear or to take an initiative before it was ready to be taken could lead only to misfortune. It was a question of taking Shakespeare's tide at the flood. He didn't want to be 'bound in shallows'. Bingham turned and retreated, much to Pippa's consternation.

Scrambling out from the wood he came upon the small, steep path that led to the beach and The Smack. He made for the bar, ordered two halves and collapsed in the corner by the window. When he looked up, the beer was in front of him and Amos Pritchard and some cronies were watching him from their usual table. It was barely 11 o'clock and there they were drinking and wishing him the worst of luck. He was a stranger meddling in village affairs that were best left to the locals.

Bingham could read the message in their eyes: go home and leave us alone.

He hadn't phoned Lina for how long? Bingham took the phone from his pocket and made the call to the house line. There was no answer. She was probably in the village somewhere or perhaps had gone into Ipswich to meet up with an old school friend. Bingham left a message, and told her he loved her. He was relieved Lina had been out: he didn't like conversing with her when he was rattled. They'd never had a row and they were too old to start now. Bingham downed the second half, checked that Pippa had drunk from her bowl and went to his room to lie down for a rest.

He knew it was late as soon as he woke, hot and sticky, with the sun shining in on him from the side window that overlooked the garden. What time had Jenny Inkpen said for lunch? Noon? Bingham looked at his watch. So much for a catnap: it was half-past twelve already. He couldn't arrive drenched in sweat, but there was no time for a shower. Bingham towelled himself down, effected a complete change of clothes and left with Pippa at his heels. He cut through the clifftop wood where the shade would keep him fresh and arrived at one o'clock.

"I'm so sorry. A catnap turned into a slumber."

"Never mind, George! You're here, and I'm sure the salad will not have wilted completely away. You do like salad? I thought I'd cook the main dish on the barbecue when you arrived. Can I get you a glass of wine?"

"Thank you," Bingham replied, disappointed that beer hadn't been offered. He didn't like mixing his drinks and he could still taste the two halves on his tongue.

"I thought I'd cook us a risotto. I had an Italian lover once – not that he was all the Italians are cracked up to be at that sort of thing – and he introduced me to the delights of Italian cuisine, even if he didn't introduce me to the delights of anything else."

Bingham heard the laugh in her voice and saw her look at him, as though waiting for a reaction. He took the white wine she offered and swirled the cool liquid over his tongue.

"Sit down, George. The risotto will take forty minutes, and I can listen to you as I cook. What do you make of our locals?"

Bingham was not to be hurried into an opinion, and he ignored the question.

"I think I have a clear picture of where everyone was at that time on that day."

"Really. You have worked hard. What are your theories?"

It was the second time she'd asked that question; theories seemed to be high priority.

"I don't have any."

"I'll refrain from repeating Gaye's response – 'I thought you were a detective'."

"Mrs Hewitt actually said, 'We thought you were a detective'. She included you in the opinion."

Bingham noticed the hand stirring the onion, garlic and rice pause for a moment.

"My, you are the sharp one, George. Are you telling me that you place significance on the difference between 'I' and 'we'?"

Bingham stood, quite suddenly, and walked across to the other side of the lawn, where he looked down at the cottage garden border: purple-leaved violets, double daisies, columbine, peonies, Vatican sage, meadow roe, campanula, geraniums and gypsophila.

"Mrs Hewitt seemed to be speaking for both of you."

"You thought we'd been talking about you, and you were offended."

"Not exactly."

"But I'm close."

"Possibly."

Bingham was barely listening. Something had clicked in his memory, but he couldn't catch the picture or the thought. He turned and smiled at Jenny.

"I'm sorry. I had a sudden image, but it's gone. One of the problems of growing old is the catching of recent memories."

Bingham watched as the asparagus and peas were stirred into the rice and Jenny ladled on some hot stock. He crossed to the table – which stood under the shade of an old beech tree and on which she'd placed the condiments, plates and cutlery – and helped himself to another glass of wine.

"Do help yourself, George. Perhaps it will stir your latent memory."

"I imagine you do have theories."

"As a writer I can postulate a number of scenarios."

It was the second time she'd made the same remark, and Bingham concluded that knowing the answers was important to Jenny Inkpen. He sipped the wine from his second glass, topped it up and waited.

"Hasn't it occurred to you that she might still be in the area?"

It had, but Bingham remained silent, watching the stock being added ladleful by ladleful and Jenny stirring continuously with the wooden spoon.

"Which of the locals are on your 'good' list, George, and which are on the 'bad'?"

"I'm not inclined to rush to judgement."

"He who hesitates, George."

"'Understand and judge not': the words of a French writer. I can't remember who, but I'm sure he or she is more or less right. I might change it to' understand before you judge', but that's my right wing coming out."

"A child of eleven is taken by a husband and wife and kept in a shed at the bottom of their garden for eighteen years. During that time she has borne her abductor two children. Does that surprise you, George?"

Jenny Inkpen raised her eyebrows and gave Bingham a knowing look, as though she realised he was out of touch with any event of the past ten to twenty years.

"A girl in her early teens is snatched on the way home from school and kept locked in the basement of a house in the middle of one of the most sophisticated cities in the world. She is forced to have regular sex with her abductor who allows her the occasional wander in his garden. It is during one of these 'outings', years later, that she finds the gate open and escapes."

Jenny removed the risotto from the heat and stirred in the shredded mint.

"I believe that Natalie Beddoes is either in such an outbuilding not three miles from her home or in such a basement in one of your local towns."

She grated Parmesan over the risotto and carried the dish to a table set by a pond, where large goldish darted in and out of the stems of the water lilies. Jenny smiled as she served Bingham and invited him to help himself to the salad when he was ready.

Bingham was inclined to comment that neither supposition offered any lead as to where Natalie might be or who might have been responsible for her abduction, but he refrained from doing so.

"You trust people, don't you, George. You're a naif in a world of the sophisticated. You cannot imagine that the Beddoes themselves might be involved or our bucolic vicar and his wife or that rough diamond, Amos Prichard, or – as I have indicated before – the sister and her boyfriend. You need to look closer to home, George."

"There is no evidence to suggest that any of these people are involved with Natalie's disappearance. It's the wisdom of the gutter press, the gossip of the corner shop or the tittle-tattle of ladies who lunch."

"Do I detect a misogynist at my table, George?"

"Quite the contrary: I liked both Emma Beddoes and Eileen Crisp."

"It's well-established that a ruthless man has a powerful influence over sensitive women."

"I've often found it to be the other way round."

If Bingham had intended to offend Jenny Inkpen, he could not have succeeded more effectively than he did with this remark.

"I am a successful writer, George, and might add that I have far more experience in matters of crime and the criminal mind than I imagine you possess. I have studied both criminology and psychology at my own expense and in great depth for many years."

"And that's what brings you to Aldewich?"

"Yes. I'm researching a book on rural crime. The working title is *Bucolic Bastards*, but I imagine the publishers will want that changed."

"And you were hoping to feature Natalie's story?"

"I visited when she disappeared six years ago, and so I have all the action of the initial investigation, but I didn't move down here until a couple of years later."

"You kept your presence quiet at the time: no one mentioned you. Why move here?"

"It's convenient for London – a train from Ipswich or straight down the A12 – and it's handy for my research. I write about current crime. I'm not interested in regurgitating something that happened a hundred years ago."

"Did you know the Tilts before moving here?"

"Why do you ask? Oh, I see – you're theorising."

"No. I don't. Remember? But you are avoiding answering the question."

"We've met up occasionally. Her husband has some link with the publishing world. I'm not sure what. I met them at the launch of my second book, *The Rapist of Lyon*."

"And Gaye Hewitt?"

"Gaye's just a country girl who has a romantic view of the arts world. You can hardly blame her – stuck out here. She's bright and takes an interest in films, theatre, books – you name it – and so she enjoys the conversation when we get together."

"What do you know about her son's father?"

"I'm not sure I should be telling you this, George. She's my friend. He's no longer on the scene, and hasn't been for many years."

"Where does he live?"

"Abroad. Holland, I think. She met him on a day trip or some such jaunt and – you know what bastards men are?"

"Some of us – maybe. Does her son know his father?"

"No, I don't think so. It's a long time ago. Gaye doesn't talk much about him. He was just a bang in the night. You've had a quiet, uneventful life, haven't you, George. Things have ticked along more or less smoothly: perhaps the occasional hiccup but nothing to rattle the cage. It's not like that for everyone. People like Gaye make one mistake with one bastard, and they're left to pick up the pieces and soldier on. Luckily, she's a trained nurse and specialises in midwifery. A job for life, you might say."

"When you were here at the time, did you make any enquiries at the monastery?"

"Ah, you're thinking of religious perverts, are you?"

"No, but they can't be dismissed."

"The domestic staff is small in number and they were all very busy since those on the retreat had just had lunch. I couldn't pin down which of the guests was where, but none of them would have taken out a car for a drive because isolation was the point of the retreat and leaving the premises was not allowed. The only one on the move was the gardener – and guess who that was – Mr Marjoram, who comes rough and ready but cheap and cheerful."

"You'd like to think he was involved, wouldn't you?"

"It would certainly make a good story. It'd make an even better one if it was his son."

Bingham had found himself warming to Jenny Inkpen, but her remark led him to despise her and himself for doing so.

"Don't hold me in disdain, George. We all have to make a living in this wicked world, and people enjoy reading about crime, especially when children are the victims."

Chapter Seven
LYING OR CONCEALING THE TRUTH

Bingham had enjoyed his lunch with Jenny Inkpen, and reflected on this as he made his way home – or what passed for home at the moment. Overcome as he was by the wine, Bingham only realised he was at the end of that particular footpath when he reached it.

It was time to take the walk, now; he knew this to be so. Pippa went slightly ahead, sniffing and looking back to see he was following. Once on the track, Bingham wondered why he'd hesitated. It was, to all appearances, only a footpath: it led nowhere, it gave no answers. Was that what had caused his fear – that he would find no answers, even on the last ride Natalie Beddoes had taken? Was the footpath going to tell him to go home, insist he was an old man, out of his depth and out of time?

The path was exactly as he had seen it in his mind's eye: the rough hawthorn hedge to his left, the padlocked gates to his right and the quiet hum of people beyond the gates, the excitement of the two black Labradors when they sensed Pippa's approach. He called her back; he wasn't ready, yet, to reach the end of the path.

Bingham placed his eye against the locked gates and wondered. Had Natalie ever reached the end of the footpath? Had her last journey ended nearer to home? Was it simply that the bike had been dumped where

Natalie's grandmother found it? His view through the woven fence showed a long garden stretching away towards the wood and the clifftop. The corner of a bungalow was just visible.

There was no pattern to the siting of these gardens: one went in one direction while another was quite differently angled, but each must border on that of the grandmother, Gwen Davis. How secret were they, one from another? How sure where the police that no one was at home in either of the first two gardens? Of course they were sure! Bingham had no doubt that the official search had been thoroughly executed.

Bingham looked to his left across the meadow of Whitefriar's where the Tilts pastured their horses. People had been crossing the meadow at the time, according to Brockie: a family with two, black Labradors. They had neither seen nor heard anything of note. Bingham looked at the locked gate. It was securely rutted in long grass and earth, and no one could have opened it, locked or otherwise. At least not now, but how was the path six years ago?

It was a cold trail he walked; Bingham was aware of the futility of his investigation. Investigation! He gave a dry laugh. It was directed only towards him, but he still felt ashamed. One shouldn't give up – not ever. Pippa looked at him, sensing his change of mood. Was there reproach in her eyes? He thought so, and his laugh softened.

Bingham walked on and came to the garden of the Labradors. Were they still there? Something had attracted Pippa, and he found her sniffing at the noses of two of her kind: older now and with grey hairs round the mouths, but undoubtedly the two who had last seen

Natalie Beddoes while their family sat at lunch. If only dogs could talk.

It was moments later that Bingham found himself at the end of the footpath and standing on the stretch of gravel by Gwen Davis's gate. It was here where she'd found the wheel of her granddaughter's bike still spinning. Staring down at the patch of ground, so ordinary and yet so tragic in its aspect, Bingham remembered he'd phoned one of his daughters to ask how long the wheel of a fallen bike would spin. He wondered why Cecilia hadn't called back, and then remembered he'd switched off his phone. Thank goodness for voicemail, he thought, and took the phone from his pocket. Cecilia's voice showed a similar irritation to Lina's when she'd been unable to contact him.

"Dad, there's no point asking people to phone you if you insist in switching off your phone. We tried your experiment several times with Bruno's bike and that of his friend. Whether the wheel spins depends on the type of bike. On Bruno's the pedal has to be free, which it isn't if it's trapped against the ground where the bike's fallen. This meant it didn't spin at all. But on his friend's bike the wheel spun for about twenty seconds, sometimes less. I hope that's helpful. Bye, Dad and love."

His daughters always ended a message sending their love, whatever their tone had indicated, while his sons never did, but they never sounded annoyed with him. Bingham rang back and thanked Cecilia, wishing her the same on her voicemail.

'Twenty seconds'? Whoever Natalie's abductor or abductors were they certainly moved with a speed that was nothing short of incredible. Bingham looked along the driveway. If she was anything like her daughter, Gwen

Davis would expect him to speak with her. Bingham heard his feet crunching the gravel.

Before he reached the door, Gwen Davis had emerged through it, a little lady, wizened by age, wisps of grey hair fluttering across her forehead to be brushed aside with the back of her vein-lined hand. Bingham wondered how old she might be, and then realized – given the age of her daughter – that Gwen Davis was probably no older than him; but she looked it, worn down by worry and guilt.

"Mr Bingham? I'm so pleased you have come. Will you find our Natalie? I blame myself. I shouldn't have … I was only seconds away from her."

"Twenty or less – to be as precise as we can, Mrs Davis. How do you do. Are you sure the wheel was still spinning?"

"I don't know, anymore. I seemed to remember that it was. Is it so important, Mr Bingham?"

"George. Call me George. It might be, but whether or not the wheel was spinning there is no doubt that you were out here very quickly, and yet heard and saw nothing."

"Nothing. Natalie might have disappeared into thin air."

"Not even the sound of a car?"

"No, but my hearing isn't good."

"Join the club, Mrs Davis. But you would have noticed movement, wouldn't you?"

"Yes. I saw nothing."

Not for the first time during his investigation, Bingham found himself short of questions. This little, old lady had been on the toilet when her daughter phoned; Bingham assumed 'in the bathroom' was a euphemism. How long had she really taken to reach her gate? In the panic of those few minutes, how clear were the mother's and daughter's notions of time? And if the wheel hadn't really been spinning, then 'seconds' would have become 'minutes': not many, but enough.

"What did you do when you saw Natalie's bike on the ground?"

"I picked it up. I don't know why. Don't ask me. It seemed the natural thing to do, and I placed it against the gatepost. I even picked up the jar of chutney and put it back in the basket."

'Put it back in the basket' so that everything was in order and back to normal. Bingham smiled to himself.

"I don't find that so strange, Mrs Davis."

"Call me Gwen. Please call me Gwen."

Listening to the anguish in her voice, Bingham was glad he wasn't a police officer. How difficult it must be to remain detached in such circumstances? Already, he wanted to put his arms around her shoulders to bring some comfort, while an official investigation required objectivity and an ear for the facts.

"Can you remember whether or not you looked up and down the road before you went back in and phoned your daughter?"

"It was the first thing I did. I thought Natalie might be on the road and was worried she might get knocked over. I looked up the road to Easleton and then down to the beach. She wasn't there."

"And there was no sign of any vehicles?"

"No. Can I get you a cup of tea, Mr Bingham?"

"No, no thank you. I've just had lunch."

Bingham looked at his watch. Lunch had been over an hour ago. It was close on four o'clock. He must have stood on that footpath a long time.

It was at that moment a ball landed by his feet. When he saw it, Bingham was conscious there had been a quiet thud-thud while he'd been talking with Gwen Davis. He hadn't paid much attention to it: the sound of a ball being kicked against a fence had simply been part of the background sounds. There was nothing odd about it, any more than the scraping of pebbles on the beach or the fluttering of birds as they flew in among the leaves of a tree.

"It's young Joe Hewitt. He'll be along to fetch his ball in a moment. I always tell him to just come round and get it. I don't always hear the door."

The boy paused in the gateway when he saw Bingham. Was it nervousness or caution? Bingham wasn't sure, but he knew boys well enough to realize that this one was belted in tight.

"You've a good kick on you, son," he said, but still the boy didn't smile.

Bingham picked up the football. He could have simply booted it towards the boy, but Bingham wanted him to come and get it. Eventually, Joseph Hewitt shuffled along towards them, and Bingham handed him the ball.

"Here, Joe," said Gwen Davis, as she drew a wrapped toffee from her apron pocket.

The boy smiled but kept his eyes on Bingham.

"Do you play in the school team?"

"We don't have one. It's a small school."

"A village school, Mr Bingham," explained Gwen Davis, "They go to the big school when they're eleven."

"Of course. I'd forgotten. Do you like school, Joe?"

"It's all right."

"You have plenty of friends?"

"Some, but they don't live here. They live in Easleton and Middleham and Leiston."

"You don't play with the village children."

The boy didn't answer, and Gwen Davis intervened.

"There aren't many children in the village of Joe's age."

"You cycle to your friends, do you?"

"Sometimes, but mum likes to take me in the car."

"And you have a kick-around. There's a playing field near the school at Middleham, isn't there?"

Bingham watched the boy's eyes widen, as though his thoughts had been scoured.

"I saw it on the map," he said with a smile, which the boy returned.

"Your mum has certainly bought you a good football. It's the right size and weight for you, isn't it?"

"Mum asked at the school. She likes to get things right."

"That's thoughtful of her. Give a workman the right tools and he'll do a better job. When I was a boy we kicked around with a grown-up's football – a heavy, leather one. On a wet day it weighed a ton."

Joseph laughed again.

"Can you head the ball?"

"I'm all right. Mum throws it for me."

They were close now to what Bingham wanted to know, but he still hedged the question, keen not to alarm the boy, keen that he shouldn't turn and run; and 'run' was in his eyes.

"Here, let me," he said and, moving back from the boy, he tossed the ball towards him, making sure that it was well placed.

The header was a good one, and Bingham was sent scuttling backwards to retrieve the ball. Joseph Hewitt laughed out loud. Bingham dropped the ball to the driveway and angled a shot towards the boy who headed it neatly downwards. Bingham caught it on his toe and slid the ball upwards. He crouched and headed the ball at the boy who trapped it precisely and gave Bingham a decent pass.

"Joe, Joe!"

They hadn't heard the car: Bingham and Gwen Davis because of their deafness and Joe because he was absorbed in the game. Gaye Hewitt stood at the end of the driveway, calling to her son. Bingham cursed quietly under his breath. He'd wanted to talk to the boy without the mother being present.

"Joe came to collect his ball," explained Gwen Davis.

"I've told him not to trouble you, Mrs Davis."

"It's no trouble. I like to talk to him once in a while. It breaks up the day."

"As long as he's not been pestering you," replied Gaye, looking sharply at Bingham.

"He's a good footballer, Mrs Hewitt," said Bingham, "He tells me he plays with his friends on the school field sometimes."

"He does when I can run him over there. I don't like him cycling. The roads aren't what they were."

Bingham cursed himself again, dismayed that he'd allowed the conversation to touch upon cycles and roads. If only he'd had the training a police officer receives, it wouldn't have happened. The anxiety he'd expected appeared in Gaye Hewitt's eyes as soon as the curse died on his tongue.

"Well, now I'm home, we'll be off. It's time for Joseph's tea."

She might just as well have said 'End of': her whole manner reeked with the dismissal. Bingham gave the boy a smile and watched them both disappear along the driveway.

"I'll have that cup of tea you offered, now, if that's convenient, Gwen."

He hadn't wanted the tea – a beer was beckoning – but there was just a chance that Natalie's grandmother might say something; besides, she needed an ear and Bingham was a good ear.

It was after five o'clock before Bingham left and made his way to The Smack. He saw nothing on the road, at least not along the fork that took him to the pub.

Tony Ship, the carter, and Amos Pritchard, the fisherman, sat at their usual table, an arm's length from the bar; with them was a third man who Bingham had not seen before. All three froze as he walked in and ordered "two halves of whatever bitter you recommend and a bowl for Pippa". Lewis Paulton didn't smile; he seemed anxious, and Bingham put this down to the conversation he'd heard between the men.

He nodded acknowledgement of their presence and sat in his customary seat on the far side of the hearth. He was thirsty; the taste of the wine lingered on his tongue despite Gwen Davis's sharp and excellent cup of tea. Watching the three men and noting their obvious hostility, Bingham pondered on the fact that it wasn't so much the members of Natalie's family who resented his questions as the other locals; and yet everyone had turned out for her special service and all had shown – or feigned – concern.

He looked closely at the third man; something in his face recalled a memory. It was a while before Bingham realized it was the face of Pete Marjoram, much older of course but the similarity in the features was unmistakeable.

"You staring at me?"

The question with its endowed threat wasn't unexpected. Staring at people was one of Bingham's faults as Lina was wont to remind him; it had become worse since his increasing deafness had introduced him to lip reading.

Marjoram rose from the table, shoving aside Tony Ship's restraining hand, and approached Bingham. His gait was unsteady; he lurched and gripped the bar for support, pausing a few feet from where Bingham sat.

"I said, you staring at me?"

"I apologise."

"What?"

"I'm sorry. It's a bad habit of mine. My wife is always ticking me off about it. We hadn't met and I wondered who you were."

"Oh, you wondered, did you?"

"Until I realized you were Pete's dad."

"You leave my Pete alone."

"I bumped into him one day. That's all," Bingham lied, remembering that Pete had asked him not to divulge their conversation with his father.

"We don't want strangers here asking questions. We want to be left well alone. The past is the past and best forgotten. You spying for the police?"

"I'm nothing to do with the police."

"That's not what I heard."

Bingham remembered, vaguely, that he had told someone of his friendship with Simon Brockie but couldn't recall the person. Gossip certainly spread quickly in the village; times hadn't changed much in such communities since he was a boy. Did that explain how Marjoram knew he'd been talking to his son? Why he was so concerned?

Bingham wasn't one to embrace commonly held 'truisms' but, at that moment, he was drawn to believe that redheaded people had a propensity for ill-temper. He hadn't been conscious of Marjoram's red hair until the man towered over him, glaring with an hostility that could only have been manufactured rather than felt. The man had no reason to hate him, but the hate was there, in the flex of his shoulders, the bursting veins of his face and the sideways glance he gave the landlord.

"Your good health," said Bingham, raising his second glass, "May I buy you a drink?"

"I don't drink with spies."

Marjoram continued staring for a moment or two, and Bingham saw the landlord move into the bar, but then the man's anger subsided as quickly as it had risen

"And nor with men who drink half pints," he added, as though it was a second thought.

With that remark he turned back to his friends, pleased to have scored one over Bingham, consoled by the fact he thought he'd done someone down. Bullies were ever such, and Bingham had handled a few in his career.

Lewis Paulton looked at Bingham and smiled, before bringing him two more half pints.

"You'd do well behind the bar," he whispered, "I have a message for you. The vicar was in earlier and asked Teresa if she'd ask you if you'd join him and his wife for dinner."

The last thing Bingham wanted was John Crisp's cheery chatter over dinner or to stumble along Eileen

Crisp's shambled hallway, but he asked Lewis Paulton to phone through a delighted acceptance for him.

Bingham felt he'd been on the go all day; he'd also missed his doze after lunch, and knew he'd never stay awake during dinner if he didn't get a cat nap. The heat, even in Jenny Inkpen's cleverly-planted garden, had got to him, and Bingham was aware that his shirt and underpants were sticking to his skin. He needed to lie down and cool off.

"Give me a shake if I'm not awake by seven, will you?" he asked Lewis Paulton, and then, followed by Pippa, staggered rather than walked up the stairs to his room.

He was, as it happened wide awake when Teresa tapped on his door; and having cooled himself with a wet flannel and found fresh clothes, Bingham made his way to the vicarage.

When Eileen Crisp opened the door, he offered a silent apology: there was no sign of any disorder. Coats were hung on the stand, shoes were stowed on the rack, umbrellas and two walking sticks were angled neatly in the stand beneath the coats and there was no sign of any children's toys littering the hallway. Instead it glistened with a fresh polish.

Moreover, Eileen Crisp was dressed as he'd never imagined her: a neat, perfectly fitted cocktail-style dress hugged her trim figure and her hair was brushed to glistening point. Gone was the harassed housewife pushing stray strands aside; in her place stood a woman poised to show off her home and her culinary skills.

"Come in, Mr Bingham. We ought to have asked you before but..."

She left the explanation hanging, shrugged and laughed. Whatever tension he'd seen in her before had vanished completely.

"Teresa says you're a vegetarian but that you eat fish. Is that right?"

"Yes."

"Good. Amos had provided me with some delicious cod."

Delicious it was: baked in parsley, low-fat yogurt and sun-dried tomato pesto and served with a fresh salad it literally melted in the mouth. They ate Eileen's meal, which was followed by a simple dish of strawberries and cream, in the vicarage kitchen, while the last rays of summer sun poured in through the skylight.

It was only after the meal, during which Eileen Crisp had elicited as much information about his private life as was decently possible, that the conversation turned to Natalie Beddoes disappearance.

"I think you must have spoken to nearly everyone who were close to Natalie or in the village at the time she vanished, mustn't you, George?" said John Crisp.

"I'll go and do the dishes while you men talk," said Eileen.

"I'd rather you stayed, Eileen," suggested Bingham, "A woman's perception in these matters is always to one's advantage."

On the lips of most men, such a comment might have sounded ironic, but there was something about Bingham's manner that conveyed sincerity; and Eileen saw him as a man who appreciated women.

"I'd like you both to consider the idea that someone, somewhere in this village knows something that will unravel the mystery of that little girl's disappearance in moments."

"You mean that someone has been lying?" asked Eileen.

"Lying or concealing the truth."

"Doesn't that amount to the same thing?"

"I don't think so, John. A man – or woman, for that matter – hears what he wants to hear and disregards the rest – to borrow a line from Paul Simon."

"You mean that someone knows something but has refused to disclose it because they can convince themselves that it's of no importance."

"Yes, Eileen."

"But that would imply a callousness beyond comprehension."

"Would it? Possibly, but it may not be apparent in the person's everyday demeanour. Most people know what goes on in slaughterhouses, but they still eat meat."

John and Eileen Crisp exchanged glances. Bingham had a tendency towards abruptness that could be embarrassing, and it had been.

"Are you asking us if we know of such a person – someone given to self-delusion?"

"I would imagine both of you know the people here better than anyone. Is there someone whose habits have changed dramatically since Natalie disappeared? Is there someone carrying an unbearable burden?"

"You'd be in a difficult position, now, if we were Catholics, dear."

John Crisp looked at his wife.

"No I wouldn't. Occasionally, George, we do hear confessions. It's not formal and there are no Hail Mary's as with our fellow Christians, but it does offer comfort to parishioners and is a better option than suicide. As with a Roman Catholic priest, I would be bound to respect the secrets of such a confession."

"Even if it involved the abduction of a little girl?"

"Even if it meant that."

"You don't mean that, John."

"I do mean that, Eileen. I would, of course, urge such a person to come forward."

The sun had died now and the skylight was dark. John Crisp felt challenged by Bingham's probing, but Eileen realised what he was doing.

"You're trying to stir our memories of that day, aren't you, George? Trying to make us remember something that might be stored at the back of our minds, something that might have struck us odd then or in the months and years that have followed?"

"Is there something or someone behaving out of character, or someone who on that fateful day and in the immediate aftermath behaved unusually, out of order, not as you would have expected?"

Bingham was trying to persuade them both to talk, to talk about people for whom they had a genuine concern, people they had come to love – in the sense in which that word is used in the Bible.

"You're both part of the village, aren't you? And yet you're both intelligent, educated people who should be able to assume a degree of objectivity. Am I right in supposing you both realized the Pecks had not been as forthcoming as truth demanded?"

"To be honest, it had occurred to us."

"Yes. If they were snogging at the top of Tony Ship's field at the moment Natalie disappeared, they must have heard something – and yet they never came forward for fear their parents would have been angry."

"I don't think either of those young people had any idea that what they might have seen or heard had any bearing on Natalie's disappearance."

"The police might have made something of it, together with other snippets of information that could have come their way."

"And you're after our snippets, George?"

"Yes."

His habitual cheeriness seemed to have deserted John Crisp. He sat at his wife's table, his face crumpled with remorse for what he might not have done. At this point, a police officer would have pressed home their advantage and the Crisps would have known what it was like to be subjected to the 'third degree'; but Bingham, too, lacked the necessary objectivity.

"I'm sorry to have put the damper on your excellent meal, Eileen. I really did enjoy it."

"No, no! Not at all, George: you've made us think. You've felt close to a breakthrough at times, haven't you?"

It was more than Bingham had dared to acknowledge lest it slipped through his fingers, but he was pleased Eileen Crisp said what she did.

"Way back, perhaps soon after I arrived, something was said that should have opened a door, but it didn't because I can't remember what it was. I'm rather like you, in fact: bound up with the people involved."

"There seemed nothing substantial in what the Pecks might have heard."

"No, John, and that's exactly the point I'm making."

Bingham left soon after. The beautifully cooked meal in the polished clean house in cheerful company had turned sour when two people and their questioner realized that someone somewhere could and should have done more to resolve the mystery of a little girl's disappearance.

Bingham avoided the bar and went straight to bed. He was in no mood for conversation. He settled Pippa, pulled up his covers and tried to sleep. But sleep wouldn't come. He heard the last customers leave, heard Teresa lock the doors and Lewis fill the dishwasher for the last time that day. For hours he tossed and turned, disturbing Pippa whenever his duvet fell to the floor. On such a night at home he would have excused himself from their bed and slept in his study rather than keep waking Lina. He would have walked down to the orchard and watched the hives in the quiet of the night or wandered beside the fields of barley and wheat. Here in Aldewich there was nowhere to go, or was there!

When he started from his sleep and looked at his watch, Bingham realized it was only two in the morning and that he was wide awake. He dressed silently and made his way to the back door followed by Pippa. After turning the key and raising the latch, he slipped out into the warm night and made his way down to the beach.

It was mild and he felt comfortable just in shirt sleeves. The shingle crunched under his feet. Bingham rested himself on the gunwales of an old fishing boat, one never to ride the waves again, and looked out at the flat sea, bronzed in the moonlight. Above him the sky was clear but for a few clouds that hung motionless. He looked at the tideline, at the driftwood and the lobster pots, at the cork floats and the tangles of seaweed baked dry from the day's sun. He listened to the water whispering on the pebbles.

Bingham didn't want to move; he gripped the boat and waited for the word to come. Only stillness could produce a memory now, a memory that had eluded him.

He felt calm and settled: the tossing and turnings of the bedroom left far behind.

He looked up and saw the lights of fishing boats somewhere out there in the stillness, the nets cast, silhouettes moving gently back and forth. In the morning their catch would glisten on the shore, gutted with the gulls screeching overhead.

A few gulls were still abroad, drifting around the boats or coasting inland on the warm, rising air, as quiet as the night, as elusive as the thought, the word, that worried Bingham. Again and again the memory came to him, only to be wisped softly away.

He must avoid any attempt to force it from his mind; the word must decide for itself when to enlighten him; it came, tapped at his consciousness and then was gone, like a gull lifted on the air. But Bingham was determined in that quiet way of his that the word would come, come and settle and enlighten.

Pippa, knowing her master well, rested at his feet, not wanting to disturb the night, attuned to his mood. The early morning light was seeping over the horizon before he stirred, tousled her ears and made his way back to the pub. Teresa was already brewing tea in the kitchen when he came in through the back door, and offered him a cup.

He smiled without speaking and sat at her table drinking it. Sensing his reluctance to engage in conversation, Teresa went about her morning routines and didn't notice him go to his room. When Bingham appeared at breakfast time, she cooked him Welsh rabbit without asking and he ate hungrily, washing it down with two cups of scalding tea.

Teresa noticed his occasional glance out of the bar window and his unusual reluctance to walk Pippa.

She was even more puzzled when he ordered toast and marmalade to follow the main breakfast.

It was only when the school bus pulled up and they heard the voices of the children that Bingham wiped his mouth on the napkin and rose from the table.

"I think it's time to pay an early morning call, Teresa," he said, "I've just got time to fetch my jacket and then I'll be on my way."

Chapter Eight
THE OTHER ROOM

"Yes, Bruges. It doesn't matter, but I'd rather not go through Amsterdam if possible. If the word brusque can describe an airport, then that airport is Amsterdam... I'm not sure, but pack a case for a few days... No thanks, Lina, not this time. I think I can manage the language, hard of hearing or not... I'll tell you later... Yes, I'm going to pay my bill now and I'll be on my way home."

Bingham was home long enough to stroke the dogs, say hello to the cats, drink the coffee and eat the eggs royale Lina insisted he needed; and then he was dozing in the passenger seat of the car while she drove him to Ipswich station, having explained that there were no direct flights to Bruges from the UK and that his best bet was Eurostar.

She refused to say farewell until she could wave him goodbye from the platform as the train disappeared into the tunnel. In that brief time, Bingham had told her nothing. He couldn't – not until he was absolutely sure of the situation.

Having been awake all night, he was shattered and slept all the way to Liverpool Street, where he was woken by a young woman who had put up with his snoring throughout the journey. He was grateful to her and to Lina's excellent planning, as he made his way like a somnambulist to Bruges: he had found all necessary tickets, a note on timings and booking confirmations placed in his wallet as well as directions to a hotel that was five minutes from the centre of the city. The fact that it had been converted from a former monastery brought no particular consolation to Bingham, religious or otherwise, but the soft bed and the clean sheets did and he collapsed and slept for several hours.

It was night when he woke, refreshed but hungry. Against his instincts to disturb anyone at such an hour, he rang for room service and was soon tucking into a dish that involved herring, potatoes, beets, apples, pickles and mayonnaise that the waiter told him was traditional cuisine. He refused the Belgian beer offered and drank orange juice instead.

The address he had obtained in Aldewich, using a blend of persuasion and threat, brought a smile to the face of the concierge.

"Achterstraat, sir? Yes. It's a residential area, you know – attractive enough in its way, but not one of our more visited sites. Turn left outside the hotel and make your way to the Market Square. Once there, ask for Ezelbrug – that's Donkey Bridge, and any local will direct you there. It's just beyond the Eiermarkt – that's the Egg Market, a popular place for tourists. Once over the bridge, you'll come to Ezelstraat – that's Donkey …"

"Street?" suggested Bingham, who was just a trifle annoyed at the young man's tone, which had become to his mind mildly patronising.

"Yes, sir, Donkey Street. It's a long one but takes you to Ezelpoort …" replied the concierge, pausing and lifting an eyebrow, before continuing, as Bingham hesitated to attempt a translation, "Gate, sir, Donkey

Gate. Beyond that you'll find a veritable maze of streets. Ask the locals."

"Your English is very good," said Bingham, having heard no one use the word 'veritable' for years.

"We speak most of the European languages in Belgium, sir."

"Yes, I'm sure. Thank you. I'll just take a stroll, I think. Good night."

"Good night, sir."

Despite the anxiety heavy within him, Bingham found the walk to be a pleasant one. How could it be otherwise, he thought, in a city as beautiful as Bruges? He'd visited many years before, followed the lapping waters of the Langerei, tasted the chocolate, sampled the beer at the Half Moon Brewery, watched the fishermen and admired the houseboats on the canals, discovered the Hof Sebrechts Park with its tranquil garden, taken a journey back in time to the Merchant's Quarter, enjoyed the views from the Rozenhoedkaai where he'd chatted to a local artist and visited the Beguinage, a safe haven for pious laywomen who chose to devote their life to contemplation and the help of the poor, in the company of a young feminist.

He went no further than the bridge, wanting only to locate Ezelstraat, and stood for a while looking along the canal, brooding on the knowledge that within every society there were always the toerags, that small percentage of people who among their decent, moral, law-abiding neighbours lived degenerate lives, the scum that society needed to skim from the state but never could; Emile Smet would be such a person.

Bingham had decided on his drive from Aldewich how he would deal with Smet should the need arise, but first a reconnaissance was in order and that must wait until daylight.

When the hour came, Bingham skipped breakfast – his night meal was still heavy on his stomach – and was soon crossing the city. Already the streets were bustling with life: a café owner was re-setting tables, a customer left breakfast in hand, a cleaner closed the side door of a solicitor's office, a white-collar worker paused to look up at the sky as she crossed the Market Square, by the side of the canal a boat owner swabbed the decks, another was swilling bilge water from the bottom of a rowing boat, a priest nodded on his way to mass, a group of children ignored him completely as they brushed past on Donkey Bridge.

Bingham was beyond Ezelpoort in no time and found himself in the concierge's 'veritable maze' of streets, although Bingham thought them anything but a muddle. The streets seemed organised on a grid pattern and though they twisted and turned into one another it was easy to move with some degree of certainty in the right direction.

Many houses seemed to be without garages and cars crowded some streets, which were free of litter. He passed a convenience store and a chemist's shop. On one corner he found a café where locals sat over coffee and toast with jam. Bingham asked for Achterstraat and was offered 'links', 'rechts'. 'rechtdoor' and 'tegenover'. He smiled and walked on, his good knowledge of German helping a little.

A woman, removing her post from the box on the wall, looked him over as he passed. Bingham smiled but there was no response except in her eyes, which noted the presence of a stranger. He noticed that many windows were shuttered, whether from the summer heat or for security he was unsure; but these houses gave the impression of being locked in tight.

Bingham's intention was to find number nineteen and watch for Smet to leave. Bingham would then attempt to gain entry to the house and see what he could find, but this would have to be accomplished discretely and he needed to find access to the back. One or two gated alleyways seemed to offer a possibility, but remaining inconspicuous would be difficult.

These were residential roads, off the tourist track, backstreet Bruges where the people of the city had their homes. He found Achterstraat with its clean pavements, and its bikes propped against the walls of the houses. A boy cycled by. Feeling foolish, Bingham avoided his eyes. A woman stood at her front door, taking the air. Bingham nodded, and repeated his discourtesy to the boy. Aware that he was now the criminal, a man fearful of meeting the eyes of decent people, Bingham hurried on.

Further along the street he found a low wall that he judged from the foliage dangling across the top hid a garden. So these houses did have gardens! That was a relief: gardens meant back doors.

Soon after the wall, Bingham came to number nineteen. It was shuttered. He observed the peeling, green paint on the door, window frames and sills. Looking quickly up, he saw that the bedroom windows were also shuttered.

At the end of the street he felt he must walk on: simply walking up and down would attract attention. Bingham had heard of police officers and private detectives keeping surveillance on a property for hours or even days on end, but couldn't imagine how they might have achieved this in Achterstraat: even a strange, parked car would attract attention.

Beyond the street, he came again to the canal, which he supposed must have twisted round in some way; houseboats lined the banks, alongside which were a wide open grassed space and a children's playground with slides and see-saws. Bingham sat down on a convenient bench and felt at home: an old man resting his feet. It was still early; soon, young mothers would arrive with their children. Back in Aldewich, mothers would be walking their children down to the school bus.

After a while, Bingham strolled along the towpath looking for a way to the back of the houses on Achterstraat. He found it more easily than he dared to hope. Having counted the houses from number nineteen to the end of the street, Bingham now counted them back again. The back gate he faced bore the same peeling, green paint. Bingham heaved a sigh of relief and tried the latch, but the gate didn't budge. He had expected as much.

Was Smet at home or had he left for work? Bingham wanted to secure his success; he needed to have a hold over Smet: the fear of involving the police. He needed lone access to the house and time to prepare.

This was the underworld, the grubby underbelly of society where the maggots lurked; and Bingham was now part of that world, like it or not.

He took the photograph of Smet from his pocket: the photograph of the man leaning against his grey van with a six-year-old boy in his arms. Surely Smet was known in the street – or was he: many people in England barely knew their next door neighbours.

Bingham decided to walk Achterstraat once more – a return journey shouldn't attract too much attention – and then he would find that little café, where the locals had been so helpful, and wait over a coffee. Perhaps Smet would pass that way into the centre of Bruges? Perhaps he might show the photograph and ask if anyone knew the man? He would wait and ponder.

But as he passed the door, Bingham changed his mind. Perhaps it was because he was thinking of children, having just sat by the playground and with the face of Natalie Beddoes ever fresh, that he suddenly remembered a game he'd played as a child: Ginger's Knock. Bingham glanced along the street, rapped on number nineteen, crossed to the opposite pavement and walked rapidly away. He turned the far corner, placed himself against the wall and looked back. No one came to the door: either Smet had left for work – or whatever occupied him during the day – or he was a very sound sleeper.

Faced with a decision, Bingham was overcome by the enormity of what he was about to do: undertake a burglary. He hesitated, and then made for the café where he joined the locals for coffee with toast and jam. Perhaps he should try to discover where Smet worked? Perhaps he should approach the man directly? Perhaps he should take what he knew to Brockie: the police would follow this through far more effectively than he would find possible – or would they? How much red tape would obstruct cooperation between two forces?

These were last minute fears. Bingham had made his decision on his way home from Aldewich, and foolish though it might now seem he intended to carry it through to some conclusion, come what may.

He avoided a third walk along Achterstraat, choosing to approach the alleyway that skirted the back of the houses along the parallel road, and came once more to the Smet's gate with its green, peeling paint. There was no point in hesitating now: either luck was on his side or it wasn't. If things went badly wrong and he was seen by a neighbour who would almost certainly report him to the police, he'd ask them to contact Brockie and share his findings.

The wall of the gate was low, and Bingham clambered over in no time, gripping the wooden gateposts for leverage. He brushed the dry lichen from his jacket and trousers and made his way quickly to the back door; once close against the back of the house, he could not be seen by anybody in the neighbouring houses, and he paused, breathless and afraid.

The familiar phrase 'in for a penny, in for a pound' came foolishly to mind, and Bingham drove his elbow swiftly through a small pane of glass by the side of the back door. It allowed him to lift the handle of the lock, open the window and climb through. He found himself in the kitchen, relieved that he was out of sight rather than fearful of what he might find.

Unwashed pots and pans were everywhere: stacked in the sink and crowded onto any available surface. Opened packets of food were spread liberally among the mess: pasta, rice and plastic trays that had once contained ready meals. The stale smell of sweat and dried juices hung in the air.

Bingham moved rapidly through to what appeared to be a sitting room. This was equally untidy and unkempt but this time with smeared screens, video games and children's toys; it was the latter that brought the first chill of the day to Bingham's heart. Dolls and cuddly bears that should have indicated innocence and joy told quite another story.

He moved quickly into the room that fronted the street, moved aside the lace curtain and peered out; the street seemed to be quiet, and Bingham sighed with relief. Quiet meant time to explore. He glanced around and realised the room might have been his grandmother's, seventy years before: furniture, ornaments and furnishings spoke of an age long past. Either Smet was a collector of bric-a-brac and retro or he was living in a home that had belonged to his family for a hundred years or more.

Bingham returned to the sitting room where he had seen the door to what he supposed was a stairway to the bedrooms. He paused with his hand on the knob. What was he going to find? Recent publicity had shown that abducted children were often kept locked in rooms or cellars for years; one girl had even been found in a shed. He hoped that Natalie Beddoes was still alive, but hadn't expected to find her quite so easily.

Bingham opened the door and put his foot on the first step. After that move it was easy, and he arrived at the stop of the stairs where doors went off to both his left and right.

The room to his left, which must have opened on to the back of the house, was in sharp contrast to the kitchen: tidiness was the order of the day. A well-padded, revolving desk chair faced a large screen to which was attached a DVD player and a video player. Behind the desk chair, backed in the corner was an easy chair, old and comfortable, in which a man could recline. Spread across the wall behind the screen was rows and rows of video cassettes and DVDs, all dated and named.

One could read about such horrors but standing among them was quite another matter. Overcome by a mixture of anger, despair and loathing, Bingham left the room for the relative decency of the landing, and his imagination quietened.

Once he'd pulled himself together, Bingham opened the door of the other room at the top of the stairs. It was set up as a recording studio. In the middle was a bed with several cameras placed around it. There was sound recording equipment of all kinds: tape recorders, computers and a Dictaphone. On a table placed in the recess of the wall behind the bed were a photocopier and an SLR camera; beside these, neatly stacked, were photographs, diaries and albums.

A second door led from this central room, and Bingham supposed it to be the front bedroom; he expected it to be locked but the door opened readily and he found a normal bedroom, untidy but not littered. He moved briefly around the room until he came to a carrier bag containing unclean tissues. He wondered why anyone should have kept such things in an otherwise tidy room; a fresh box was on the bedside table next to the bag.

Another world was opening up, and Bingham returned to the landing. He felt in his pocket for his mobile phone; if he heard movement downstairs, he'd jam one of the doors to lock himself in and phone the police. In the meantime … in the meantime, he must collect the evidence he needed, and knew he'd find that in those tapes and discs.

He stood over the desk that supported the computer screen and wondered which tape or disc to take. Did it matter: surely all would contain revolting images? But he had to be sure, had to nail this man beyond any reasonable doubt. Bingham hesitated to touch any of the discs marked 'Natalie 2009'. He reached for a video cassette of an earlier date; it bore a girl's name, 'Anna'. Just as he was about to touch the video case, the word 'fingerprints' crossed Bingham's mind, and he could not recall having brought gloves of any kind or plastic bags or even tissues. Tissues! Once more he crossed by the bottom of that bed and into the front bedroom where he took several from the clean box.

He handled the tape by its edges, snapped it into the cassette player and switched on the player and the screen. Smet was lying on the bed with a little girl on top of him and facing him. They were both naked. It was quite clear that he was trying to push his penis into the child's vagina. Most disturbing of all was the fact that Anna was reaching forward, her arms round Smet's neck as though in a loving embrace. At that moment, Bingham understood, first hand, exactly what was meant by the term 'grooming'.

With tears in his eyes and rage in his heart, Bingham turned off the tape and replaced it in the case. He selected several others, both tapes and discs, without viewing their contents, wrapping them carefully in the tissues and made his way downstairs. Admiration for those officers who were part of the Paedophile Unit at Scotland Yard welled up within him. He felt his cowardice: a police officer would have no choice but to keep viewing and Bingham knew he wasn't made of such stern stuff. What he did feel as he made for the back door was that he'd never sleep again – not peacefully, not without a nightmare or two.

He couldn't face climbing out through the window and was glad when he saw a large key hanging from a nail in the kitchen wall. He unlocked the door, leaving it so, and strode to the back gate. It didn't matter whether or not he was seen; all that concerned him was to get away. He slid the bolts on the gate, pulled it to and walked from the house in Achterstraat as fast as his legs would carry him.

Although sickened and panicked by what he'd seen in his brief glimpse of Smet's video, Bingham's mind was crystal clear as far as his intentions were concerned: he needed to secure the safety of the films. With that in mind he purchased cellophane, brown paper, bubble wrap and sticky tape from a newsagent's and made his way back to the hotel.

It took him almost an hour to wrap the two sets of the films and write covering letters. The first he placed in his hotel room safe with the letter addressed to Lina at their home; the second, he addressed to Brockie, being careful to include the policeman's former title 'DCI' in case the Belgian authorities proved to be as punctilious as the Dutch who some years before had confiscated two bottles of obviously duty free alcohol from his wife because they were in the wrong type of sealed bag.

Afternoons always found Bingham tired, and this one particularly so. He approached the concierge: this time a young woman who was as helpful but less sardonic than the young man and who was more than prepared to see that his parcel was posted safely to the UK. Being unable to face lunch, Bingham retired to his room and slept for two hours.

When he woke it was late afternoon, and Bingham knew the night to come would leave him exhausted. A shower, fresh clothes and a meal seemed to be the answer. He didn't want to eat but knew he must. Facing Smet, he would need to be on top form and hunger played no part in being fit for such a task.

The concierge – the young man again – recommended two restaurants;

"Both on Sint-Jacobsstraat, sir – the Wereldcafe de Republiek or In Den Wittencop. The former is rather bohemian but the food is always fresh and there's a large, interior courtyard, which will be very welcome in this heat. The latter is, perhaps, a shade on the retro side for your taste and the cuisine, perhaps, a trifle French, but the couple who run it also specialise in traditional Belgian food."

Bingham couldn't decide whether the young man was attempting to rile him or whether he prided himself in speaking a form of classic English, but the retro comment made him aware of how old he was and he wondered what impression he would give to Emile Smet.

Rather than be put down as past it, Bingham chose the retro restaurant and was rewarded with a dish called waterzooi. He couldn't fault the food and promised himself that he'd bring Lina here one day, but his mind never left the task he'd set himself and by the time he knocked on Emile Smet's door he had rehearsed, over and over again, the pattern he hoped the encounter would follow.

"Emile Smet?"

"Ja."

"My name is George Bingham. I visited your house this morning and removed certain tapes and discs. We need to talk."

Smet looked up and down the street and then beckoned Bingham to enter.

"Might we sit here? It seems to be the most comfortable room."

"I haven't invited you to sit at all, Mr Bingham. Where is my property?"

"We'll talk about that later. I've come to find Natalie Beddoes … and take her home."

Smet looked at Bingham as though he was listening to a lunatic, and Bingham could see the denial pursed on the man's lips; but Smet remembered the tapes, and – in particular – the one marked 'Natalie 2009' as he was about to lie.

"How did you find me?"

"It doesn't matter. You came upon Natalie quite by chance, didn't you, as you were about to leave Aldewich in your grey van? The temptation was too much, wasn't it? I imagine you shoved her into the back and drove off down the road past the church to Eastwold where your boat was waiting. Did you stop somewhere on the way to gag her? I imagine so. You'd need to arrive quietly at the quay in Eastwold and secrete her aboard. Why the boat? Were you bringing drugs into the country? Eastwold is a well-known resort for smugglers – quiet, respectable, plenty of money swilling around. Once you'd crossed the North Sea to Ostend, you made your way along the canals to here. Or did you come by road – another van, perhaps?"

"You seem to know a great deal – or imagine you do. But you're not a policeman are you?"

"No."

"So why are you sticking your nose into my business."

"I told you. I've come to take Natalie home."

"Supposing there is some truth in your speculations…"

"Don't waste time, Smet. Should your tapes and discs land in the lap of the police, you'd be finished."

"Is that likely to happen?"

"I didn't come here unarmed, so to speak. Your property, fingerprints intact, will be opened by a police officer tomorrow unless I make a phone call, and that call will not be made until I leave here with Natalie Beddoes."

"That's not possible. She isn't here."

Bingham's heart sank; he'd always believed the child to be alive. He realised Smet saw the panic in his face. The man smiled.

"You don't know what you're up against, Mr Bingham. Come upstairs. Let me show you something."

Standing in Smet's office, looking once more at the tapes and discs, Bingham felt he was at a disadvantage, despite believing he held all the cards. Smet tapped a pile of magazines Bingham had noticed but ignored.

"You see the titles – *Lolita, Young Debutantes, Teenagers from Holland, Piccolo*. I might have picked them up in Amsterdam. There's plenty of the same in that city. But I didn't. *Lolita* came from a shop in Nottingham. *Piccolo* comes from Lucca. Are you beginning to understand? We are worldwide. You are not dealing with a lone Belgian. Have you heard of the Swiss Paedophile Association? Of course not! We are organised, and we do not appreciate snoopers. Sure, you can hand me over to the authorities, and they might imprison me for a few years, but I'll be out and active again. You, on the other hand, will be dealt with. You understand me?"

Bingham was afraid. The advantage he thought to be his had vanished.

"You think I made all these films, do you? Many of them are swaps. That is the price of membership – the swap. It has to be of a certain quality, of course – not just any old swap. We all have different tastes, you see. Mine is for young girls – nothing over eight years. Others prefer those with a little more development – the small breasts, you know. A friend in Amsterdam likes the very young – a one-year-old is a joy to him …"

"That's enough, Smet. Understand that I have no intention of leaving here without Natalie or of, at least, knowing where she is. If I do not, you most certainly will go to prison, and I imagine a large section of your organisation will be exposed."

"I do not have Natalie."

"But she is alive."

"I do not know."

The two men looked at one another without speaking for some moments; both were aware that the other could deal a blow that would devastate their world. Bingham knew that Smet would want to avoid prison at all costs, while Smet knew he'd shocked Bingham into fearing for his life.

"I could destroy all this before the police ever arrived."

"How long have you been swapping these films, Smet – twenty years, thirty? You want your tapes, don't you? A collection going back decades destroyed in a moment of panic, when all you have to do is lead me to Natalie Beddoes?"

"It's not as easy as you think."

Again the silence as Smet tried to assess the odds against him.

"I haven't seen her for a long time. I couldn't keep her here and I passed her on."

"Passed her on?"

Bingham couldn't help himself. Had he been a younger man, he would have struck Smet with his fist.

"You people think we kill these children, don't you? But it's in our interests to keep them alive. They're no use to us dead. We've no time for child killers. We love these children. You don't understand that, do you? It sometimes takes years to get them to co-operate. You have to win their trust. I've never grabbed a child off the street…"

"You grabbed Natalie."

"It was a mistake – the impulse of the moment."

"How long did you keep her here?"

"Aah – you can't catch me like that. I never said I did."

"I have the tape."

"But you've not watched it otherwise you wouldn't have asked that question."

"Watching the tape of Anna was enough for me."

"I got Natalie to pose for me – that's all."

"Pose?"

Bingham could see that Smet was wondering whether he should continue the conversation along the lines it was going; he could also see that the man wanted to do so. At last, desire overcame discretion.

"She was naked, walking about the room. I gave her a bowl of warm water. She washed herself … slowly with soap. It was nice. She was uninhibited, see. There's always something attractive …"

"About childhood innocence?"

"Yeah."

"And you were making this film for somebody else?"

"Yeah – there's a market for innocence."

There was no irony in Smet's voice; he meant every word he said.

"How do you contact your market?"

"There's the net, of course, but we still use the old-fashioned ways. You know what they say – the old-fashioned ways are best. We leave our cards in certain shops – like the one in Nottingham where I got *Lolita*.

That one holds letters and forwards them. Some of us drop in for our mail once a week."

"And the mail is about swapping films?"

"Yeah."

"And that's how you contacted the man who wanted Natalie?"

"No – that was on the net."

"Go on," said Bingham, softly.

"Before I do, Mr Bingham, I want some assurances from you."

"Go on."

"Firstly, I get my films back immediately. Secondly, the police are kept out of this. Thirdly, my name's kept out of this. Fourthly, I want to know how you got on to me."

"I promise that neither the police nor whoever has Natalie will hear your name from me. I'm not prepared to pass on any names to you for the same reason – a promise. As far as the tapes are concerned, they stay with me until I've found Natalie. They are my only safeguard against you lying to me."

Smet thought for a moment: threats and persuasions were what he lived by, were what he understood.

"Let me repeat my warning, Mr Bingham. I'm not responsible for what others might do. As I said, we're worldwide. We have a long reach. If I wanted a film of an eight-year-old girl being beaten, tortured with needles, raped and then killed – not that I do, I'm not that way inclined – I could get it. Do you understand me? Someone I met in South Africa offered me one that involved a boy being beheaded by masked men … I'll give you a name and an address and trust you to keep your word and get those tapes back to me and keep your mouth shut. If you go back on your word, your life won't be worth living."

Bingham thought of Lina and his four children; he thought of his three grandchildren.

"You have my word," he said.

"Just to be clear, Mr Bingham. The tape of the little girl was made in England – on an industrial estate near Liverpool. You do understand me, don't you?"

Chapter Nine

INSTRUMENTS OF IGNORANCE

The plane carrying Bingham and Lina touched down at Pisa airport to a round of applause from the passengers and some religious crossings of the heart. The Italians aboard were grateful to have landed safely.

Lina had joined Bingham at Amsterdam, having flown from Norwich, and he'd spent the time they waited at the airport outlining his experiences with Emile Smet. Against her wishes – Lina did not like driving on Italian roads – he insisted upon hiring a car at the airport and driving to the little town of Fornaci di Coreglia, which was set in the hills of Tuscany.

"I have no idea whether Natalie is here, dead or alive, but if we find her we shall need to be mobile, Lina."

"I can see that, Bing. I've booked the Hotel Ristorante La Lanterna, by the way. It's quite central. We can't miss it."

The hotel was of the kind they always chose when in Italy: built in the middle of the nineteenth century, when the lime kilns that gave the village its name were in full swing, and having remained with the Togneri family ever since, it represented the quiet past of Lina's favourite country. Even should the La Lanterna be refurbished, it would retain the same colour scheme and furnishings throughout. Bingham smiled at his wife as they entered the foyer: the same thought had occurred to them both.

He was quite content for Lina to do the talking as Giovanni Togneri came forward from behind the reception desk and bowed his head courteously towards them. Bingham always enjoyed his wife conversing with the locals: she had the knack of opening them up, whereas his Italian, having been learned the old-fashioned way – grammar first and vocabulary afterwards – was rather stilted.

Giovanni greeted them but he was the Old Signor Togneri; it was his son, Leopoldo, the Young Signor Togneri, who carried Lina's suitcase to their suite. Suite was, perhaps, an exaggeration: they had a sitting room in addition to the bed and bath rooms as well as a kitchenette, but it was not extravagantly spacious, although the balcony that looked out over the town centre added an attractive dimension.

Lina brewed a coffee and they sat drinking while Bingham pondered over the rough plan he had in mind. Lina knew better than to disturb him at such moments, and sat watching the locals hurrying about their daily business. The prime mode of transport seemed to be scooters – the type popular in Britain during the sixties; young and old alike glided by as she watched. Across the road, a young woman served iced coffees to customers who sat in the shade, away from the oppressive heat of the Tuscan summer. A policeman wandered by, noting everything, doing nothing but chatting to the locals. Along the road out of town, daily market stalls were selling fresh vegetables, fruit and smoked meats. From below, Lina could hear the voices of people who sat drinking in the La Lanterna bar.

"It's hard to believe that evil exists in this lovely place," she said.

"I thought the same in Bruges, until I met Emile Smet. There's nothing we can do today, Lina, but accept Giovanni's invitation to dine here. Tomorrow morning, I want to drive up to this hamlet in the hills. It's the address I eventually obtained through Smet."

"And you are sure he wasn't setting you off on a wild goose chase, Bing?"

"No, I'm not. He might simply have been playing for time, but he had nothing to gain by doing that and everything to lose. I told him that I would release his tapes and discs to the police if he had lied to me. However, he didn't actually drive Natalie here. The contact was a man in Amsterdam. They leave cards for each other in known shops – known, that is, to men of their kind.

"Smet told me in that gloating way of his that I'd bitten off more than I could ever chew. He was secure in the knowledge that their web operates worldwide, that while the police are running round in circles every one of them knows where a missing child might be. You remember the little girl who was taken from that camp site on the French coast some years ago?"

"Yes, she'd only wandered down to fetch water for her mother."

"Smet told me that one hundred and forty children had disappeared along that stretch of coastline over the previous ten years. Not many, is it? One point four children a year doesn't attract too much attention, but none of them has ever been found, which means they may well be alive – and we know what that means."

After an early breakfast, Lina found she was clinging tightly to her side of the car while Bingham negotiated the narrow, twisting road that they needed to traverse on their way to the hamlet of La Sereni. Rock falls were evident and numerous. Several times, Bingham left the car parked while he cleared a path. He dreaded approaching vehicles: the road was barely one track. The local farmers seemed able to pull over and perch on the very edge of the precipitous valley sides, but Bingham possessed no such confidence. Soon they were lost and wondering, such were the number of tracks that led off from the main road.

"We should have taken the bus," said Lina as they passed a stop situated on the corner of a hairpin bend.

Bingham cursed silently, but refrained from answering. Just past the bend, he took a track to the right and found himself in the driveway of a hill farm. A young man, busy hoeing some vegetables, looked up and smiled. Bingham nodded to his wife, and Lina climbed out of the car.

Lina was attractive in the way women in their sixties are when they outshine a younger person. There was the smile, the mane of black hair she'd refused to have cut as an acknowledgement of her age and the high cheekbones; but it was more than mere appearance: there was something about her eyes and the experience of life shining from them that drew younger men. The farmer propped his hoe against the fence and came over, his face lit with a smile that matched Lina's. Bingham listened, pleased to hear his wife doing the talking.

"Giuseppe would like us to share a coffee with him."

"Yes, he *would*."

"Don't be coarse, Bing."

Under normal circumstances, Bing would have enjoyed the moment: coffee brewing as only the Italians can brew it in a Bialetti pot, homemade pastries that Giuseppe brought from a tin on the dresser.

"My mother bakes for me. She brings me a tin once a week."

Lina was in her element, laughing and joking with the young man while Bingham listened. The ritual must take its course, and there no way in which Bingham would have been rude enough to hurry it on.

"Giuseppe wants us to see his pig," said Lina, giving her husband a smile that only he saw.

Giuseppe's pig was kept in a small outhouse built with the local stone and the young farmer explained how it was his pride and joy, fed only on the best of fresh vegetables and fruit in addition to its regular meal. While they watched, he brought a bucket of glistening, green apples from the kitchen, obviously cut while they waited judging from the white flesh, and fed them lovingly to the pig that snorted with pleasure.

"He will taste very good when he is ready."

Bingham looked at Lina and they both smiled, resignedly, at the cruelty inherent in the world.

"Before you go."

Giuseppe walked back into his farmhouse and brought a brown bag stuffed with the wild fungi of the hillside and forest.

"For you."

They could leave now; the ritual of the welcome drink for the stranger was satisfied. With the social chit-chat also out of the way, Bingham felt able to ask the question he'd been harbouring since they arrived.

"We're looking for La Sereni," he said, "and a man called Pietro Salvi. Would you know him?"

Giuseppe's face it up.

"Si. Pietro. He was once a lawyer in Coreglia, and now lives with his granddaughter at La Sereni. He drinks at the Lanterna bar. Sometimes he goes there to meet his granddaughter from school, but often she comes home on the bus."

"The bus goes to La Sereni?"

"Twice a day – once in the morning and once in the afternoon."

"Is Signor Salvi at home today?"

"I imagine so. I haven't seen him come along the road. If he had, he would have called in."

"The girl has no mother?" asked Lina, glancing at her husband.

"The mother left when she was a young woman. There isn't much here for the young. She must have died because Pietro's granddaughter came when she was five or six, and now he looks after her. They are devoted to each other. When she came she didn't speak a word of Italian. Can you imagine that – an Italian mother who does not teach her child her own language?"

"Did you ever meet her – the mother?"

"She was very bright – unlike me – and she went to a different school. They lived in Garfagnana then."

"What is the little girl's name?"

"Not so little now – hmm! She is growing fast. Her name is Alessandra."

"How old is ... Alessandra?"

"She will be ... eleven, perhaps twelve."

Back in their hire car, Bingham turned to Lina.

"We have no need now to go to La Sereni – at least you don't."

"You're sure that 'Alessandra' is Natalie?"

"The age matches as does the address Smet gave me. I'm taking us back to the town, and I want you to be at the bus stop when Natalie arrives to go home from school. Try and attract her attention – even if you have to board the bus to do so. Show her these photographs that Emma Beddoes gave me on my last morning in Aldewich. They are of Natalie six years ago, of course, but she will hopefully remember herself as she was at six years old, and she will remember her mother. Don't panic her, Lina. Remain calm."

"You don't need to tell me that, Bing. It has also occurred to me that she may not remember a word of English."

"Yes… and that's an even more pressing reason why you must meet her. I had expected – no, hoped – that we might find her in Sereni but this will be so much better. We – you – can gain her confidence away from Salvi. These men have a stranglehold over their victims. What she has been doing for him, she will have been convinced she is doing for a loving friend. If anyone can win her over, you can, Lina. You're as good with children as you are with young men."

"And what will you be doing?"

"Once I've dropped you in Coreglia, I'm going back to La Sereni."

"There's no need for you to go, now."

"Yes, there is. Don't worry about me, Lina. You'll have enough on your plate."

Driving back to Sereni Bingham wasn't sure why he needed to do so; at least, that is what he told himself. It might have been more sensible simply to have remained at the hotel until some kind of official assistance had been summoned; but Bingham wanted to meet Pietro Salvi. At the back of his mind there were answers to be gained, a score to settle. He would have preferred

Lina's skills with him, but she was needed elsewhere; he wondered whether Salvi spoke English.

He reached Sereni in the early afternoon by which time the Tuscan sun was beating down unmercifully on the village. The houses were spread out over the hillside. Bingham estimated that the population couldn't be more than two hundred people, and he wondered what the inhabitants found to do all day. Did they work in Fornaci di Coreglia? Were they retired? Were the houses owned by foreigners such as the English?

He followed a dark passageway from the roadside, where he'd parked the little Fiat, to a shamble of side streets that led, eventually, to the remains of a fortress and tower at the top of the hill. From here, Bingham looked down on Coreglia, situated in the valley of the River Serchio between the soft, green Apennines and the rocky Apuan chain with its marble quarries. The town was medieval and still retained its centre where you could wander for ages between the bunched houses, delighted to lose your way, emerging eventually to some piazza where the quiet pleasures of sitting, eating and talking were abundant.

La Sereni possessed the same charm on a smaller scale. As Bingham left the old walls he came upon a little piazza almost hidden among the houses and apartments. How strange it must have been for Natalie Beddoes to have arrived here in this maze of confused buildings, among an unknown people speaking an unknown language: strange and terrifying, with no one to whom she could turn. Bingham took the piece of paper on which he'd written Salvi's address from his pocket.

He strolled down several flights of steps consisting of stone slabs cut into the hillside and came to the Church of San Felice. The door was open and Bingham walked in hoping to find a priest. In the darkness he saw nothing except a candle burning in a niche along one wall. He walked over and lit two: one for his mother and one for Lina's. It was a custom of hers to light a candle in memory of the departed, and so Bingham obliged.

Either the light or his movement caused a stirring in the church, and Bingham turned to see an elderly woman kneeling at prayer in one of the middle pews; her head was covered with a black shawl. Not wishing to disturb her, Bingham left quietly and was blinded by the sun, which seemed to bounce up from the paving slabs as well as down from the blue sky.

After only a short while, the woman joined him, a sad smile on her face until he asked:

"Do you know the house of Signor Salvi?"

Her face lit up.

"A kind man, a very kind man. He does so much for the church."

She beckoned Bingham with a tiny crook of the finger to follow her, and soon he was standing on the terrace outside a house whose paint looked fresh and whose window boxes bloomed. Bingham nodded in gratitude and stood waiting. He was unsure for what he waited, but it seemed almost impertinent in the midst of the stillness that enveloped the whole village to knock on a door.

When he did, it was opened by a man who Bingham judged to be in his sixties and at the prime of his old age. The white hair was thick and lustrous as was the moustache that adorned the man's upper lip. He was tanned quite naturally, and the bronzed face smiled at Bingham from over the whitest shirt he had ever seen.

"Signor Salvi?"

"Si."

The smile broadened. Pietro Salvi was every inch the handsome Italian, the kind that turned the heads and hearts of woman of all ages. Bingham looked down at the silver-grey trousers, immaculately creased, and the brown, patent leather shoes that shone with polish.

He was taken in, and admitted as much. He had made a mistake. Giuseppe the farmer had directed him to the wrong Pietro Salvi or Emile Smet had drawn the name from a hat.

"Do you speak English, Signor Salvi?"

"A little. I prefer my own language in my own country."

Wishing Lina was with him, Bingham said in his classic, if stilted, Italian:

"My name is Bingham, George Bingham, and I've come to take Natalie home to her family."

"Natalie? I think you have come to the wrong address, Signor Bingham."

Pietro Salvi smiled as he shut the door, giving Bingham a slight nod of the head. As the door closed in his face, Bingham rapped again and again. The sound of the knocker rang out across the little piazza. The door opened and Bingham stepped inside before Pietro Salvi could protest. Within seconds, he was standing in Salvi's elegant and highly polished hallway with the door shut behind him.

"I should like to sit down," he said, "We have much to talk about."

"You have no right to be here. Please leave my house."

"In time."

"I shall call the police if you refuse to leave."

Bingham walked by Salvi and into the man's sitting room: the marble floor sparkled, the wooden furniture shone, cushions were plumped, curtains hung in perfect folds, a coffee table on which Bingham observed magazines of the countryside was obviously set at a particular angle to the easy chair by the fireplace. In the corner of the room, concealed discretely by the chimney breast, was a television set. It was viewable from the small settee. Bingham saw Salvi and Natalie sitting there, side by side.

"I have the name of the man who brought Natalie to you."

"Natalie? My granddaughter's name is Alessandra. Please leave my house. You have no right here."

"Cornelius Molen is the name I have on the card."

"The card? What card is this?"

"The card I was given by the man who abducted Natalie Beddoes."

"Who is this man?"

"I am not able to tell you."

"Are you a policeman?"

"No, but it was a policeman who set me on the trail of Natalie."

"The police! They are merely instruments of ignorance."

"What ignorance would that be, Signor Salvi?"

Pietro Salvi looked at Bingham, who surmised that the man was wondering whether to continue. The silence remained unabated. Bingham sat quietly and waited, as he had waited so many times when a child was sent to him for some wrongdoing – imagined or otherwise.

"You believe that this Natalie is my granddaughter, Alessandra?"

"Yes."

"Where is Alessandra?"

"Is she not at school?"

"That is what I believed."

"But my presence here gives you reason to doubt?"

"Your presence here is unwelcome."

"But you hesitate to call your police?"

"I have no wish to create a disturbance."

"And no wish to explain who Alessandra might be – a child abducted six years ago from an English village?"

"You are living in a world of fantasy, Signor Bingham."

"If you believe that to be true, why not call your police officers and have me ejected?"

Bingham imagined that Pietro Salvi must be wondering exactly how much was known about Natalie and her whereabouts. It was early afternoon, and it would be sometime before the bus arrived.

"You believe I am involved in this abduction?"

"When did Natalie arrive in La Sereni?"

"Alessandra came to me ... perhaps five or six years ago. My daughter died."

"So I understand from Guiseppe, the farmer, but he had never met your daughter. He only knows what he was told by you. I am not a police officer but they would be in a position to check these matters. There would be records. I have traced Natalie here from her home in England. There is a trail of names that brings her to your door, Signor Salvi. It was here in La Sereni that Natalie Beddoes disappeared. Do you not think it will be easy to find out whether your granddaughter is or is not Natalie Beddoes once they have examined my evidence?"

Bingham sat quietly and waited, hoping his stillness might provide a spur. Salvi sat on the settee opposite Bingham and rested his head in his hands. He must be worried: the last thing he would want was a public outcry against him. Salvi obviously held a position of respect within his community.

"I have no knowledge of any such child, but I do have an academic interest in these matters. You seem to be an educated man, Mr Bingham, and yet you share the general ignorance."

"What ignorance do I share, Signor Salvi?"

"The ignorance regarding a child's sexual needs."

Bingham wasn't quite sure whether or not he had heard this correctly.

"Do you have a point of view, Signor Salvi?"

"I would argue the political case – the need for the rights to a new sexuality society does not understand. I assume a man like you has no objection to the gay community?"

"No."

"Precisely so, and yet gay men and lesbians struggled for centuries to have their sexuality legalised and normalised. Now it is the turn of adults whose preference is to have sex with children."

"And you would consider that normal?"

"Children are very sexual beings who enjoy sex. Often they take the leading role in the sex they have with adults. It is their own needs they are meeting. They have their preferences. Children are attracted to nice people: they do not like monsters. Every time I read about such things in the papers, it is always the same. We are always portrayed as sinister people, grabbing children from the streets, but it isn't like that at all."

"We?"

Bingham smiled to himself despite the conversation, amused at how that one little word had opened the way: first, in leading him to Tuscany and now in acknowledging Salvi's personal interest over his academic pose.

"You count yourself among the liberal minded, Signor Salvi?"

"It takes time… there is friendship involved."

Bingham could not deny he was fascinated. Here was a man who Bingham was now certain had held a child from her parents for six years using phrases like 'there is friendship involved'.

"If she was not willing then …"

Bingham either missed the rest of the sentence or misunderstood the meaning Salvi was trying to convey but it sounded like:

"… I wouldn't do it."

"So your way was to get to know her, gain her trust and know she was willing before any intimacy?"

"Yes, always," replied Salvi, looking at Bingham as though he had, at last, found someone who understood.

"And we are talking of your granddaughter … under your control?"

Salvi didn't answer. He stood and walked to the window, and looked out over the tumble of houses where his neighbours lived. Bingham decided to push home the question.

"But under your control? Is that why you changed Natalie's name?"

Salvi didn't answer.

"Was that to distance her from her family?"

Bingham sensed a tension in the man's neck muscles; beyond control, his shoulders twitched. Bingham had seen the like before, when dealing with a boy who knew himself to be in the wrong.

"Have you ever been married, Signor Salvi? Do you have children of your own?"

"No. I find it difficult to have a relationship with another adult."

"So you have no daughter."

"No… Ah."

"The name you chose for Natalie – Alessandra – does it have any special meaning for you?"

"It is so feminine, and it rolls off the tongue so beautifully."

"And it means 'defender of mankind'. You would know that, wouldn't you, Signor Salvi? Did it hold a special irony for you?"

"You are very knowledgeable, Mr Bingham."

"What made you choose Alessandra?"

"You don't understand, do you? We share enjoyment together, we share interests, we play games – Alessandra is good at the game you call netball. I like her company, her conversation, her childish way of looking at things …"

"Have there been others?"

"In the past but not since Alessandra came to me."

Again a phrase that implied consent – 'came to me'. Bingham had the image of a little girl running towards a loving grandad.

"It isn't just about … the sex?"

"I have never harmed Alessandra. We share a mutual pleasure."

"Does anyone else know of your secret?"

"No. It is between me and Alessandra. We share the life of the town – La Coreglia – but to everyone we are grandfather and granddaughter. Until the world wakes up it must be that way."

"There is no presumption of innocence?"

Salvi hadn't looked at Bingham since going to the window, but now he turned, the old look in his eyes, the look of the sophisticated man of the world.

"You have the capacity to hit the nail on the head, Mr Bingham. Society must acknowledge the right to be different, the right for all to choose their own way of life."

"Was Natalie Beddoes free to choose?"

"None of the men I have referred to would condone the abduction of a child for that child to be abused – raped, murdered, what you will. Such people are not … lovers of children; by definition they are not lovers of children. We do not threaten children. We do not coerce them. We are not cruel. Such men should not be at liberty. Have I said anything you do not understand?"

It was the first time since Bingham had forced his way into the house that Pietro Salvi had raised his voice.

"You see yourself as the innocent victim of a conspiracy? You believe that sexual acts between you and Natalie are consensual?"

"Don't mock me, Mr Bingham. I am not a man to be mocked."

"You spoke of getting to know Natalie …"

"That is not her name."

"You spoke of gaining her trust and of knowing she was willing before sex became involved? Would the word 'manipulation' be appropriate?"

"You are like the rest – demonising a relationship you do not understand."

"I am picturing the wits and experience of a grown man being pitted against the innocence of a child."

"That word again – innocence!"

"How can a six-year-old consent to sex?"

"I have invested my whole life in Alessandra, my time, my money ... We have a close relationship. I have given her my one hundred percent attention. I have broadened her horizons, bought her nice clothes, seen to her education ..."

"And so she trusts you because you are everything to her – all she has to protect her and take care of her?"

"Yes."

"You are in control? Your relationship with Natalie is your mutual secret?"

"We have no other choice."

"And so you involve a child in a conspiracy against other adults, against your community, against her own parents?"

Salvi didn't answer. He sat, a crumpled figure, on the settee he shared with Natalie. Bingham wondered which emotion was controlling him at that moment: fear, anger, self-pity.

"She must trust in you because you are all she has? But in the end aren't you betraying the very trust you say you took so long to establish?"

"That's a big 'but'!"

"Is it? Isn't everything you have ever done to seduce this child been done for you rather than her?"

Bingham chose that moment to take a photograph from his pocket. It was one of those given to him by Emma Beddoes on that last morning. It showed Natalie as a six-year-old sitting proudly on her little bike. Bingham handed it to Salvi.

Natalie's family life had been easy for Salvi to block out, since he had never known the actuality of its existence; but the sight of Natalie, in all her innocence, astride the bike was something he couldn't ignore. For a second,

Bingham thought he was about to rip the photograph to pieces and he rose slightly from his chair to intervene, but Salvi threw it from him, his face twitching in spasms.

"If you only opened your mind, you would understand."

"Would your community understand?"

There was a brief pause before Salvi answered. Bingham thought that perhaps he had misunderstood the remark. Pietro Salvi did not answer.

"You blend in very well do you not, Signor Salvi – a man of distinction in a society that loves children, a man generous to his church, a kind man?"

"Yes."

"I am not a psychologist, but isn't that person what is called your alter ego?"

Salvi seemed to have withdrawn completely into himself. Crouching rather sitting on the settee he looked pathetic. For a brief moment, Bingham almost felt sorry for him.

"What you *choose* to be is concealed from your community by what you *appear* to be. Am I right?"

Salvi did not answer.

"Did you give Natalie Beddoes a choice? Had she chosen to return home, would you have allowed her to do so?"

Still Salvi did not answer.

"Have you wondered what her mother and father might be thinking, what images might be passing through their minds? Has that ever concerned you, Signor Salvi?"

Salvi frowned, looked at Bingham and then at his watch.

"Alessandra will be home soon. The bus is due. I must meet her."

"I'll walk with you."

The sun was lower in the sky as the two men walked through the tumble of passageways to the path leading to where Bingham had parked his car. When they reached the open road, little more than a track against the dusty hillside, Bingham looked back at La Sereni with its quaint houses, its fortress, its tower and the church of San Felice.

A monument set into the hillside told him that this had been the last stronghold of the partisans who had fought against the Allies during the last war. As he read its words, the bus pulled in beside his car. A group of women emerged, their shopping baskets bulging with produce from the market in Coreglia. They called out in unison:

"Buonasera, signor Salvi."

"Buonasera, signore."

They inclined their heads, a puzzled look in their eyes as they gazed politely at Bingham. One of the women approached Salvi, confidentially.

"Dove Alessandra?"

Salvi smiled and shrugged his shoulders. He was clearly expecting to meet his Alessandra but she did not step down from the bus and he was unable to explain why.

When Bingham drove off and looked into his rear view mirror, he saw an old man standing in the settling dust, waiting for a granddaughter.

Chapter Ten
CONTROL OVER HER LIFE

"How is Natalie?" asked Bingham when Lina came in through their kitchen door.

"It will be a long haul, Bing, but she seems brighter, more ready to talk. The counsellor is a wonderful woman."

"Better her than me. I don't think I'd know where to start. Would you like a cup of tea?"

Lina laughed. It had been three months since they returned with Natalie and delivered her safely into her mother's arms. Lina had intended to visit the child every week, but it had turned out to be more often because her suspicions that Natalie might have forgotten her native tongue had proved to be correct, and Lina had acted as translator. Sometimes Bingham had accompanied her and sometimes not, but each time she arrived home from a solo visit Bingham offered her a cup of tea.

Their return had been swift: a call to Brockie, a visit from the consul and they'd found themselves on a flight home with Natalie minus a passport. It was the first time Bingham had passed through Border Control without having to remove his belt and shoes.

Once on home soil, officers from the Paedophile Unit had interviewed Bingham but allowed Natalie to return immediately with her mother to Aldewich. Emma and

Alan Beddoes, meeting their daughter at Heathrow, had been beside themselves with joy. Bingham and Lina smiled aside the gratitude as the child – a little girl again – fell into her mother's arms. Alan Beddoes stood watching, an undemonstrative man coping with his happiness.

Bingham had been grateful for the official help that followed: the speedy response of the Paedophile Unit, the sympathetic de-briefing, the provision of an experienced counsellor for Natalie, the support of a female officer for the Beddoes.

Ex-DCI Simon Brockie had received the news of Natalie's escape with a mixture of relief, thankfulness, admiration and annoyance.

"What was the breakthrough, George?" he'd asked a dozen times, but Bingham had always refused to be specific as he had with the Paedophile Unit.

"Salvi has led you to Smet and to a worldwide ring of toerags – be grateful. If you want to know more look at your own officers' reports at the time of Natalie's disappearance."

"We could charge you with obstructing the course of justice," DCI Jack Spencer from the Paedophile Unit had suggested.

"Yes you could, couldn't you, and wouldn't it look good in the papers? 'Private detective who found Natalie Beddoes after the police failed to do so in six years is charged with obstructing the course of justice'."

The officer gave a sigh of resigned discretion.

"I promised Smet I'd not give his name and return his tapes, which I did, while anticipating that you'd trace him through Salvi but I'm saying no more about how I found Smet for similar reasons."

"There was a promise involved?"

"It entailed more than a promise."

And Bingham would say no more.

"Very well, Mr Bingham, we'll have to respect your decision, but if you should change your mind …"

"I won't."

"No."

"Tell me, Jack, what's your view of people like Smet and Salvi? I imagine you're subjected to horrors beyond the belief of normal people. I've every admiration for what you do, knowing I couldn't stomach the work myself."

"We receive regular counselling and what you might call sabbaticals – additional time off. I never take the work home with me. I never talk about it at home. If we need to get it out of our systems, we'll have a drink after work.

I've worked in the Vice Squad. I've seen the things adults get up to in pornography. I've had what you might call 'a good grounding'. I don't see how you could do the work otherwise: coming to it straight would be staggering – seeing what adults can actually do to children.

What we need is to be taken seriously. The crimes against children we investigate are on the increase. These people go to prison, maybe for only a short time. They fester in their cell and then come out again, and they've had no treatment. No one's tried to get to the bottom of the problem. And they're not going to seek treatment for themselves.

As an ordinary policeman all I can do is try to get a conviction and have them locked up to protect the public for the time they're inside. Sometimes I think they'd be better off on a sex offenders' treatment programme.

But it does affect you. If you try to deny that, you're kidding yourself. You might say that if the sexual abuse of children doesn't have an impact on you then it really has got to you. When we start, everyone is shown what's called 'the briefing tape'. It prepares you for the kind of thing you're going to see over and over again. It shows the violent rape of an eight-year-old girl by a man in his fifties. You can't imagine the images and sounds in that film."

Bingham had not slept for nights after his discussion with Jack Spencer; he rose quietly from bed and went to his study, where he sat wondering how on earth anyone was going to bring Natalie Beddoes back from what she'd endured.

He and Brockie would meet apart from their wives, perhaps to share a drink, perhaps just to chat over a cup of coffee; but the talk always returned to Natalie and her abduction.

At one such meeting, Brockie took a sheet of paper from his wallet and handed it to Bingham.

"Jack Spencer thought you'd want to read this. It's from Salvi's diary. I hope it helps you understand these people better. He was meticulous, was your Signor Salvi. The original is written in beautiful cursive script. There's an entry almost daily, but this one is particularly interesting."

Bingham unfolded the sheet of paper and read:

'I have control now. I have taken away her control over her own life. Each time I have her, I force my needs on her. I manipulate how she thinks, how she behaves and how she acts; not just towards me but towards everybody. I did this by

shunning her, by denying her affection so that she would always come to me for attention; then, I would lavish her with love, until she needed more.

I make her feel guilty and confused; I make her feel responsible for making me happy. In that way, I make it impossible for her to turn to anyone for help. I make her feel that she is complicit in the acts, that she wants the love, that she is as needful as I am needful. Confusion follows and her control of her own life is gone and she is in my hands.'

"That's how these people break into a child's mind, George – what the public call 'grooming'. The nicer they are the less chance there will be of the child telling what has happened. Natalie was groomed to the point where Salvi was able to send her to school without having any qualms that she might tell, even after she'd learned the language."

"I'd often wondered why such victimised children didn't talk about the abuse earlier."

"And now you know – these men confuse the child about what is happening, they make the child feel the guilty one, they make the child feel that it is their needs that are being satisfied. These men have a powerful hold over their victims, George: adults, abused as children, find it very difficult to come forward and reveal the truth of what happened to them."

When Bingham arrived home afterwards he took Lina in his arms and kissed her.

"What's that for?"

"It's for being the only person in the world who could have persuaded Natalie not to board the bus that day."

Bingham handed her the sheet of paper from Brockie's wallet.

"Read that and you'll see what I mean."

Lina's next visit to Natalie occurred during what the papers called 'a cold snap' in November, and Bingham went with her. A thin, almost transparent layer of snow covered everything. The roads had been churned clean but late into the morning the silver birches, the gorse bushes, the bracken, the roofs of cottages and the overhead wires along the road to Aldewich were all laden with snow that was beginning to disperse so that small drops of melt water glistened as they fell.

Lina parked on the car park by Percy's fish restaurant. Releasing their three dogs from the hatch, they walked across the snow to the shore line. The gunwales and nets were also hung with snow, although the salt on the pebbles had cleared the beach. After the dogs had enjoyed their run and a rub down, Lina and Bingham walked the clifftop path to Emma Beddoes' house.

"Mr Bingham ... Lina, oh do come in. I've got some coffee on for you Mr Bingham. I know you like coffee at this time, and the kettles boiling for tea for you and me, Lina. Alan's up at the farm. He'll not be back 'til lunchtime but I know he'd like to see you. I've some fresh-baked scones nearly ready in the oven."

Bingham sat at the kitchen table, thankful for Natalie that among the horrors of her life, here, at last, was a normality she must have hoped for so many times.

"Natalie and Moira are out walking. Moira's been a different girl since Natalie got home, and the lady who counsels Natalie – Mrs Landers – is wonderful. I didn't like to interfere at first but ..."

At that moment, Emma Beddoes burst into tears. Lina cast a warning glance at Bingham and put her arms round the younger woman.

"I'm sorry ... It's just unbelievable what she's been through ... but it's best out in the open. Natalie needs to talk it out. I knew it would be difficult. I often wondered if we'd ever cope should Natalie return to us, but I just knew that if we got her back we'd pull through it together. I don't want her damaged. I want her to have a normal life. Whatever we have to face we face as a family."

"How's Alan taking it?"

"As best he can, Mr Bingham. He was frightened at first, frightened to put his arms round his own daughter. He's never been a touchy-feely person but he nursed them in his arms when they were babies ... but he felt embarrassed – I think that's the word – with Natalie when we got her back."

"I think that's natural enough, Emma. He's a man and he's ashamed that one of his own sex could behave as he did; but people like Salvi aren't men – not in the real sense of the word."

Bingham sniffed and glanced at the oven.

"Are your scones ready, Emma? I'm ready for them."

"Thank goodness you noticed. We've caught them just in time."

The conversation settled to the chatter of a normal coffee time and Emma relaxed. Bingham was on his third scone and second coffee when Natalie and Moira pushed open the kitchen door. Moira went straight to the fridge, but Natalie ran to Lina and threw her arms round her neck. Bingham was pleased to see the comfort between them.

"Do I get a hug?" he asked.

There was moment's hesitation – after all, the girl had seen Lina more often – but Natalie came over and let him put his arms round her.

"How's the diary coming along?" he asked.

"You remembered?"

"It's a few weeks since I've been, I know, but remembering things is one of my specialities – even if the recall takes me a while sometimes. Was it a good idea to keep the diary? Did Mrs Landers approve?"

"She said it was something she was going to ask me to do."

As she spoke and smiled, Bingham was taken by Natalie's prettiness: the dark and curly hair, the snub nose, the bright button eyes and lips so red they'd never need adornment. That was the outside, of course – the part the world would see – but what was the inside like? How damaged was her soul and mind? Would she ever want to have a family of her own? Would she – like her mother – enjoy little ones running around her feet? Bingham remembered the pleasure his children had brought when they were young and hoped it would be the same for this child when she became a woman.

"Would you like to read it?"

"I'd like to read it very much. Just the bits you want me to read."

Natalie came back from her bedroom with her diary.

"You can read what you like, Mr Bingham. I want you to know. I don't want everyone to know but I want you and Mrs Landers to know."

Bingham looked at Emma Beddoes and saw in her eyes that it was more than she could bear to read her daughter's diary.

"One day, Mr Bingham, perhaps one day."

Bingham opened the book. The handwriting was a beautiful cursive script. Most of the entries were written in Italian, although some of the more recent ones were in childlike English. Bingham flicked through the pages, not wanting his eyes to settle on any particular paragraph, as frightened as Emma Beddoes at what he would read. He looked at Natalie and saw the need in her eyes. Turning to the first pages, he read extracts as they came to him:

He made me feel dirty. I didn't know what he was going to do to me or ask me to do to him. Even though I'm safe I still worry all the time. I worry about being taken away. I worry about someone hurting me. If another little girl was sexually abused I would tell them to tell an adult. They should talk about everything with their counsellor. I know I'm safe now with my family. I try to be brave.

He made me touch him on his private parts. He put his hand over mine. He moved my hand up and down. He kept looking at me in a certain way.

Mum and Dad got me back to school right away. They wasted no time. Mrs Landers said that was best. It was a different school to the one in the village. The children were bigger and they didn't all know me. The teacher was kind. She showed me where I could put my coat and sat me at the front of the class. I liked PE and music and drama. I thought everyone was watching me, even the teachers. Mum told me that people were afraid I would run away and that was why.

I don't want people to know what happened to me because it's none of their business. Some girls were whispering about me last week and I was upset.

Grandad seemed hurt sometimes and I had to tell him that I loved him. I had to think of the right things to say to grandad. He kept me locked away at first. When he let me out I didn't know whether it was safe. Was he playing a trick on me? What would happen when I went upstairs? Grandad would play 'what if' games with me. What if I was free? What if people talked to me?

I would often wake to find grandad hanging over me, talking off my nightdress. He would lie next to me and rub up against me and touch me. Then he would make me touch him. He would tell me what to do. Sometimes he would take my hand and show me. Sometimes he would turn me over and rub his thing on my bottom. Sometimes he would make me sit on top of him. When it was finished he would take me to the bathroom and watch me clean myself.

Sometimes I pretended to be asleep. I thought if I pretended to be asleep he would leave me alone. I have memories of waking up with my nightie soaked. I hadn't wet myself. Grandad had raped me while I slept. He always spoke in whispers. He had a very soft voice.

Grandad would come to me, but he never looked me in the eye. My breathing would quicken and my stomach churned over. I tried not to think about it and stared at the bedhead or covered my eyes. I thought if I just was still it would be over more quickly. Get it done with. I thought if I fight him he might like it and it would make things worse. If I let him he wouldn't do it anymore. When he'd finished there was always silence. He told me I gave off a scent and it excited him.

"You know that none of this is your fault, don't you, Natalie?"

"Yes. Mrs Landers has told me that many times. And she's told me that I'm wise beyond my years, but that now I need to be silly and playful and to be hugged and not to be bothered. She says I must learn to trust people again like I did when I was a little girl."

"Your friend, Mrs Landers, is a very wise lady," said Lina.

"Bing, you never did tell me what it was that led you to that man Smet."

"No, I didn't. You're such an honest person that I didn't want to put you in a position where you might have to lie. You hate lies, don't you – even fibs. It's probably your Catholic upbringing."

"Probably, but you can tell me now can't you?"

They were sitting at their own table in the farmhouse kitchen, Lina with a glass of dry, white wine and Bingham with a small beer, watching the cats preen themselves and then depart through the flap for the night. Both had been silent on their return from the Beddoes: silent with a small sense of relief. Lina had a cod they'd bought from Amos Pritchard that morning roasting in the oven.

"Something had been nagging at the back of my mind. It was something someone had said, something I'd accepted at the time but which struck me as odd later, but I couldn't recall the comment. When I was having lunch with Jenny Inkpen it almost came back to me, but then vanished. I couldn't sleep that night. I tossed and turned but eventually gave up and went down to the beach with Pippa. It was there that I remembered. It was one word – 'we'."

"We?"

"Yes. Gaye Hewitt had said 'We'd just finished our lunch and I was clearing away the dishes', but I knew her son Joseph had his lunch at The Smack and so I wondered who the 'we' referred to. She hadn't mentioned anyone else to the police, and so I waited until her son had caught the school bus and I went to see her. She blustered, of course – Gaye Hewitt is very much an 'end of conversation' type when she's had her say – but I was having none of it and told her straight that she could tell me or the police.

She confessed that she'd had lunch with Emile Smet. She was his mistress and he was the father of her child. They'd met in Amsterdam when she and some girlfriends went over for a hen party or something. Whenever he was over here he popped in for a bit of how's-your-father."

"Why was he here?"

"Eastwold is well-known as a place where it's easy to get drugs into the country. Smet would arrive on his boat, moor on the staithe, drop off his load and pop in to see Gaye."

"But she never mentioned him to the police?"

"No, she said she didn't think it was important – rather like the Pecks hearing a vehicle when they were

165

doing whatever they were doing at the top of Tony Ship's field."

"And Smet had a vehicle?"

"Not just any vehicle. It was a grey van, and a grey van was one of those things unaccounted for at the time. Smet kept it in a lock-up at Eastwold. I suppose he used it to deliver his drugs. It was the clincher me for, of course. He must have left Gaye Hewitt's after lunch just as Natalie was cycling to her nana's house. It was an opportunity Smet couldn't resist."

"And the Hewitt woman had no idea that he was a paedophile?"

"I shouldn't think so. She gave me his address in Bruges after I'd promised not to tell him or the police who'd given it to me."

"But if she had no reason to think it was him who might have abducted Natalie why didn't she tell the police?"

"Exactly! I asked her the same question and got the usual bluster about not wanting to get involved. I don't think many of her neighbours knew about Smet."

"She's an accessory to child abuse, Bing, whether she likes it or not. If she'd spoken up at the time, the police would almost certainly have waylaid Smet and Natalie would have been spared years of torment and horror."

"I know."

"So why haven't you reported her?"

"You know the answer to that question."

"Joseph Hewitt?"

"Yes. If she goes to prison or even if she's only subjected to an investigation and a suspended sentence, who will suffer most? The boy will, at the best, know what a vile person his mother is; at the worst, he'll be put into care while she serves her time. He's fourteen and has enough to handle just growing into adolescence."

"Nevertheless, it doesn't seem right."

"It isn't right."

They sat in silence. Bingham poured Lina another glass of wine, while she took the roast cod from the oven, transferred it to warm plates and added the tomatoes she'd cooked with the fish; the juices flowed into the baby potatoes and kale. They ate in silence, but at the end of the meal Lina said:

"There is one more thing that puzzles me, Bing."

"Go on."

"I've always wondered why you wanted to talk with Salvi."

"Did my concern for Joseph Hewitt put you in mind of that?"

"Yes."

"I thought so. You can imagine how much more difficult – not to say, impossible – it would have been for Natalie had Salvi been tried for his offences in a court of law. You can imagine the meal the papers would have made of what she'd had to endure, the prurient interest of the general public? It was far better that he should do the decent thing – if that's the appropriate phrase for such a vile creature."

"When you left him, did you know he might hang himself?"

"No, but I hoped he would."

Summer and Autumn 2015

ACKNOWLEDGEMENTS

Although this story is a fiction, its key events and descriptions are based on the actual incidents and experiences of people involved in similar situations and circumstances. Anyone wishing to delve deeper into the real world from which this novel is drawn should read:

The Hunt for Britain's Paedophiles by Bob Long and DCI Bob McLachlan:

Hodder and Stoughton 2002

Help Me by Katie Beers with Carolyn Gusoff:

Title Town Publishing/ Virgin Books 2013

All the characters in the book are fictitious, and any resemblance to persons living or dead, is purely coincidental.